P9-CRW-883

Branch

SPACESHIPS
& SPELLS

Also edited by
Jane Yolen, Martin H. Greenberg,
and Charles G. Waugh

Dragons & Dreams

SPACESHIPS & SPELLS

A collection of new fantasy and science-fiction stories

Edited by

Jane Yolen,
Martin H. Greenberg
& Charles G. Waugh

——————————————— HARPER & ROW, PUBLISHERS ———————————————

Cambridge, Philadelphia, San Francisco, Washington, London, Mexico City, São Paolo, Singapore, Sydney

NEW YORK

Library of Congress Cataloging-in-Publication Data
Spaceships and spells.

    Summary: A collection of thirteen original fantasy and science
fiction short stories by such authors as Bruce Coville,
Isaac Asimov, and Jane Yolen.
    1. Fantastic fiction, American. 2. Science fiction,
American. [1. Fantasy. 2. Science fiction. 3. Short
stories] I. Yolen, Jane. II. Greenberg, Martin Harry.
III. Waugh, Charles G.
PZ5.S738 1987   [Fic]   87-175
ISBN 0-06-026796-8
ISBN 0-06-026797-6 (lib. bdg.)

For all our children—
who keep us wondering!

Contents

SPACESHIPS
& SPELLS

Introduction

Why is it that we have linked spaceships and spells? The easy answer is that a person from our past—say in Shakespeare's days—would have considered a spaceship a machinery of magic. As Shakespeare's Macbeth says:

> *Can such things be,*
> *And overcome us like a summer's cloud,*
> *Without our special wonder?*

Those of us who have long loved science fiction and fantasy stories know that there is such a little difference between the magical and the mundane if one is willing to set aside the mind's shutters and simply let the light of wonder shine in.

Try this: Sit in front of a mirror and pretend it is a magic mirror, and ask your reflected self the following questions. What would it be like to own a time machine so that you could see what you are going to be when you grow up? What would it feel like to have a wish you know can come true, but only *one* wish? How would you handle a set of parents who felt that you were only capable of learning to dance, smile, and simper at handsome princes like any proper princess? How would you react if your friends called you crazy because you could hear voices, wonderful voices, calling to you in the wind and the rain?

Those are magic-mirror wonderings indeed. And yet . . . we all think about growing up and worry about our futures. We all desire wishes, lots and lots and lots of them. We all chafe at the restrictions placed upon us by our families. We all fear the laughter that might shatter our most private dreams. There is such a thin line, you see, between the magical and the mundane, the neverwhere and the everywhere.

So here are thirteen tales to stretch your sense of wonder. Some of them deal with spaceships, some of them deal with spells, and all of them deal with our very human ability to make a story out of magical reflections—and that is magic, indeed.

A Wish Named Arnold

by Charles de Lint

Marguerite kept a wish in a brass egg, and its name was Arnold.

The egg screwed apart in the middle. Inside, wrapped in a small piece of faded velvet, was the wish. It was a small wish, about the length of a man's thumb, and was made of black clay in the rough shape of a bird. Marguerite decided straight away that it was a crow, even if it did have a splash of white on its head. That made it just more special for her, because she'd dyed a forelock of her own dark hair a peroxide white just before the summer started—much to her parents' dismay.

She'd found the egg under a pile of junk in Miller's while tagging along with her mother and aunt on their usual weekend tour of the local antique shops. Miller's was near their cottage on Otty Lake, just down the road from Rideau Ferry, and considered to be the best antique shop in the area.

The egg and its dubious contents were only two dollars, and maybe the egg was dinged up a little and didn't screw together quite right, and maybe the carving didn't look so much like a crow as it did a lump of black clay with what could be a beak on it, but she'd bought it all the same.

It wasn't until Arnold talked to her that she found out he was a wish.

"What do you mean, you're a wish?" she'd asked, keeping her voice low so that her parents wouldn't think she'd taken to talking in her sleep. "Like a genie in a lamp?"

Something like that.

It was all quite confusing. Arnold lay in her hand, an unmoving lump that was definitely not alive even if he did look like a bird, sort of. That was a plain fact, as her father liked to say. On the other hand, someone was definitely speaking to her in a low, buzzing voice that tickled pleasantly inside her head.

I wonder if I'm dreaming, she thought.

She gave her white forelock a tug, then brushed it away from her brow and bent down to give the clay bird a closer look.

"What sort of a wish can you give me?" she asked finally.

Think of something—any one thing that you want— and I'll give it to you.

"Anything?"

Within reasonable limits.

Marguerite nodded sagely. She was all too familiar with *that* expression. "Reasonable limits" was why she only had one forelock dyed instead of a whole swath of rainbow colors like her friend Tina, or a Mohawk like Sheila. If she just washed her hair and let it dry, *and* you ignored the dyed forelock, she had a most reasonable short haircut. But all it took was a little gel that she kept hidden in her purse, and by the time she joined her friends down at the mall, her hair was sticking out around her head in a bristle of spikes. It was just such a pain wearing a hat when she came home and having to wash out the gel right away.

Maybe that should be her wish. That she could go around looking just however she pleased and nobody could tell her any different. Except that seemed like a waste of a wish. She should probably ask for great heaps of money and jewels. Or maybe for a hundred more wishes.

"How come I only get one wish?" she asked.

Because that's all I am, Arnold replied. *One small wish.*

"Genies and magic fish give three. In fact, *everybody* in *all* the stories gets three. Isn't it a tradition or something?"

Not where I come from.

"Where *do* you come from?"

There was a moment's pause, then Arnold said softly, *I'm not really sure.*

Marguerite felt a little uncomfortable at that. The

voice tickling her mind sounded too sad, and she started to feel ashamed of being so greedy.

"Listen," she said. "I didn't really mean to . . . you know . . ."

That's all right, Arnold replied. *Just let me know when you've decided what your wish is.*

Marguerite got a feeling in her head as though something had just slipped away, like a lost memory or a half-remembered thought; then she realized that Arnold had just gone back to wherever it was that he'd been before she'd opened the egg. Thoughtfully she wrapped him up in the faded velvet, then shut him away in the egg. She put the egg under her pillow and went to sleep.

* * *

All the next day she kept thinking about the brass egg and the clay crow inside it, about her one wish and all the wonderful things that there were to wish for. She meant to take out the egg right away, first thing in the morning, but she never quite found the time. She went fishing with her father after breakfast, and then she went into Perth to shop with her mother, and then she went swimming with Steve, who lived two cottages down and liked punk music as much as she did, though maybe for different reasons. She didn't get back to her egg until bedtime that night.

"What happens to you after I've made my wish?" she asked after she'd taken Arnold out of his egg.

I go away.

Marguerite asked, "Where to?" before she really

thought about what she was saying, but this time Arnold didn't get upset.

To be somebody else's wish, he said.

"And after that?"

Well, after they've made their wish, I'll go on to the next, and the next . . .

"It sounds kind of boring."

Oh, no. I get to meet all sorts of interesting people.

Marguerite scratched her nose. She'd gotten a mosquito bite right on the end of it and felt very much like Pinocchio, though she hadn't been telling any lies.

"Have you always been a wish?" she asked, not thinking again.

Arnold's voice grew so quiet that it was just a feathery touch in her mind. *I remember being something else . . . a long time ago. . . .*

Marguerite leaned closer, as though that would help her hear him better. But there was a sudden feeling in her as though Arnold had shaken himself out of his reverie.

Do you know what you're going to wish for yet? he asked briskly.

"Not exactly."

Well, just let me know when you're ready, he said, and then he was gone again.

Marguerite sighed and put him away. This didn't seem to be at all the way this whole wishing business should go. Instead of feeling all excited about being able to ask for any one thing—*anything!*—she felt guilty because she kept making Arnold feel bad. Mind you, she thought. He did seem to be a gloomy sort of a genie when you came right down to it.

She fell asleep wondering if he looked the same in whatever place he went to when he left her as he did when she held him in her hand. Somehow his ticklish, raspy voice didn't quite go with the lumpy clay figure that lay inside the brass egg. She supposed she'd never know.

*   *   *

As the summer progressed they became quite good friends, in an odd sort of way. Marguerite took to carrying the egg around with her in a small, quilted, cotton bag that she slung over her shoulder. At opportune moments, she'd take Arnold out and they'd talk about all sorts of things.

Arnold, Marguerite discovered, knew a lot that she hadn't supposed a genie would know. He was up on all the latest bands, seemed to have seen all the best movies, knew stories that could make her giggle uncontrollably or shiver with chills under her blankets late at night. If she didn't press him for information about his past, he proved to be the best friend a person could want, and she found herself telling him things that she'd never think of telling anyone else.

It got to the point where Marguerite forgot he was a wish. Which was fine until the day she left her quilted cotton bag behind in a restaurant in Smith Falls on a day's outing with her mother. She became totally panic-stricken until her mother took her back to the restaurant, but by then her bag was gone, and so was the egg, and with it, Arnold.

Marguerite was inconsolable. She moped around for days, and nothing that anyone could do could cheer her up. She missed Arnold passionately. Missed their long talks when she was supposed to be sleeping. Missed the weight of his egg in her shoulder bag and the companionable presence of just knowing he was there. And also, she realized, she'd missed her chance of using her wish.

She could have had anything she wanted. She could have asked for piles of money. For fame and fortune. To be a lead singer in a band like "10,000 Maniacs." To be another Molly Ringwald and star in all kinds of movies. She could have wished that Arnold would stay with her forever. Instead, jerk that she was, she'd never used the wish, and now she had nothing. How could she be so stupid?

"Oh," she muttered one night in her bed. "I wish I . . . I wish . . ."

She paused then, feeling a familiar tickle in her head.

Did you finally decide on your wish? Arnold asked.

Marguerite sat up so suddenly that she knocked over her water glass on the night table. Luckily it was empty.

"Arnold?" she asked, looking around. "Are you here?"

Well, not exactly here, *as it were, but I can hear you.*

"Where have you *been?*"

Waiting for you to make your wish.

"I've really missed you," Marguerite said. She patted her comforter with eager hands, trying to find Arnold's egg. "How did you get back here?"

I'm not exactly here, Arnold said.

"How come you never talked to me, when I've been missing you all this time?"

I can't really initiate these things, Arnold explained. *It gets rather complicated, but even though my egg's with someone else, I can't really be their wish until I've finished being yours.*

"So we can still talk and be friends even though I've lost the egg?"

Not exactly. I can fulfill your wish, but since I'm not with you, as it were, I can't really stay unless you're ready to make your wish.

"You can't?" Marguerite wailed.

Afraid not. I don't make the rules, you know.

"I've got it," Marguerite said. And she did have it, too. If she wanted to keep Arnold with her, all she had to do was wish for him to always be her friend. Then no one could take him away from her. They'd always be together.

"I wish . . ." she began.

But that didn't seem quite right, she realized. She gave her dyed forelock a nervous tug. It wasn't right to *make* someone be your friend. But if she didn't do that, if she wished something else, then Arnold would just go off and be somebody else's wish. Oh, if only things didn't have to be complicated. Maybe she should just wish herself to the moon and be done with all her problems. She could lie there and stare at the world from a nice, long distance away while she slowly asphyxiated. The would solve everything.

She felt that telltale feeling in her mind that let her know that Arnold was leaving again.

"Wait," she said. "I haven't made my wish yet."

The feeling stopped. *Then you've decided?* Arnold asked.

She hadn't, but as soon as he asked, she realized that there was only one fair wish she could make.

"I wish you were free," she said.

The feeling that was Arnold moved blurrily inside her.

You what? he asked.

"I wish you were free. I *can* wish that, can't I?"

Yes, but . . . wouldn't you rather have something . . . well, something for yourself?

"This *is* for myself," Marguerite said. "Your being free would be the best thing I could wish for, because you're my friend and I don't want you to be trapped anymore." She paused for a moment, brow wrinkling. "Or is there a rule against that?"

No rule, Arnold said softly. His ticklish voice bubbled with excitement. *No rule at all against it.*

"Then that's my wish," Marguerite said.

Inside her mind, she felt a sensation like a tiny whirlwind spinning around and around. It was like Arnold's voice and an autumn-leaves smell and a kaleidoscope of dervishing lights, all wrapped up in one whirling sensation.

Free! Arnold called from the center of that whirly-gig. *Free free free!*

A sudden weight was in Marguerite's hand, and she saw that the brass egg had appeared there. It lay open on her palm, the faded velvet spilled out of it. It seemed so very small to hold so much happiness, but fluttering on tiny wings was the clay crow, rising up in a spin that twinned Arnold's presence in Marguerite's mind.

Her fingers closed around the brass egg as Arnold doubled, then tripled his size, in an explosion of black feathers. His voice was like a chorus of bells, ringing and ringing between Marguerite's ears. Then with an exuberant caw, he stroked the air with his wings, flew out the cottage window, and was gone.

Marguerite sat quietly, staring out the window and holding the brass egg. A big grin stretched her lips. There was something so *right* about what she'd just done that she felt an overwhelming sense of happiness herself, as though she'd been the one trapped in a treadmill of wishes in a brass egg and Arnold had been the one to free *her*.

At last she reached out and picked up from the comforter a small, glossy, black feather that Arnold had left behind. Wrapping it in the old velvet, she put it into the brass egg and screwed the egg shut once more.

*　*　*

That September a new family moved in next door with a boy her age named Arnold. Marguerite was delighted, and though her parents were surprised, she and the new boy became best friends almost immediately. She showed him the egg one day that winter and wasn't at all surprised that the feather she still kept in it was the exact same shade of black as her new friend's hair.

Arnold stroked the feather with one finger when she let him see it. He smiled at her and said, "I had a wish once. . . ."

The Improper Princess

by Patricia C. Wrede

Linderwall was a large kingdom, just east of the Mountains of Morning, where philosophers were highly respected and the number five was fashionable. The climate was unremarkable. The knights kept their armor brightly polished (mainly for show—it had been centuries since a dragon had come east). There were the usual periodic problems with royal children and uninvited fairy godmothers, but they were always the sort of thing that could be cleared up by finding the proper prince or princess to marry the unfortunate child a few years later. All in all, Linderwall was a very prosperous and pleasant place.

Cimorene hated it.

Cimorene was the youngest daughter of the king of Linderwall, and her parents found her rather trying. Their first six daughters were perfectly normal princesses, with long, golden hair and sweet dispositions, each more beautiful than the last. Cimorene was lovely enough, but her hair was jet black and she wore it in braids instead of curled and pinned like her sisters'.

And she wouldn't stop growing. Her parents were quite sure that no prince would want to marry a girl who could look him in the eye instead of gazing up at him becomingly through her lashes. As for the girl's disposition—well, when people were being polite, they said she was strong-minded. When they were angry or annoyed with her, they said she was as stubborn as a pig.

The king and queen did the best they could. They hired the most superior tutors and governesses to teach Cimorene all the things a princess ought to know—dancing, embroidery, drawing, and etiquette. There was a great deal of etiquette, from the proper way to curtsy before a visiting prince to how loudly it was permissible to scream when being carried off by a giant. (Linderwall still had an occasional problem with giants.)

Cimorene found it all very dull, but she pressed her lips together and learned it anyway. When she couldn't stand it any longer, she would go down to the castle armory and bully the armsmaster into giving her a fencing lesson. As she got older, she found her regular lessons more and more boring. Consequently, the fencing lessons became more and more frequent.

When she was twelve, her father found out.

"Fencing is not proper behavior for a princess," he told her in the gentle-but-firm tone recommended by the court philosopher.

Cimorene tilted her head to one side. "Why not?"

"It's . . . well, it's simply not done."

Cimorene considered. "Aren't I a princess?"

"Yes, of course you are, my dear," said her father with relief. He had been bracing himself for a storm of tears, which was the way his other daughters reacted to reprimands.

"Well, I fence," Cimorene said with the air of one delivering an unshakable argument. "So it is *too* done by a princess."

"That doesn't make it proper, dear," put in her mother gently.

"Why not?"

"It simply doesn't," the queen said firmly, and that was the end of Cimorene's fencing lessons.

When she was fourteen, her father discovered that she was making the court magician teach her magic.

"How long has this been going on?" he asked wearily, when she arrived in response to his summons.

"Since you stopped my fencing lessons," Cimorene said. "I suppose you're going to tell me it isn't proper behavior for a princess."

"Well, yes. I mean, it isn't proper."

"Nothing interesting seems to be proper," Cimorene said.

"You might find things more interesting if you applied yourself a little more, dear," Cimorene's mother said.

"I doubt it," Cimorene muttered, but she knew better than to argue when her mother used that tone of voice. And that was the end of the magic lessons.

The same thing happened over the Latin lessons from the court philosopher, the cooking lessons from the castle chef, the economics lessons from the court treasurer, and the juggling lessons from the court minstrel. Cimorene began to grow rather tired of it.

When she was sixteen, Cimorene summoned her fairy godmother.

"Cimorene, my dear, this sort of thing really isn't done," the fairy said, fanning away the scented blue smoke that had accompanied her appearance.

"People keep telling me that," Cimorene said.

"You should pay attention to them then," her godmother said irritably. "I'm not used to being hauled away from my tea without warning. And you aren't supposed to call me unless it is a matter of utmost importance to your life and future happiness."

"It *is* of utmost importance to my life and future happiness," Cimorene said.

"Oh, very well. You're a bit young to have fallen in love already; still, you always have been a precocious child. Tell me about him."

Cimorene sighed. "It isn't a him."

"Enchanted, is he?" the fairy said with a spark of interest. "A frog, perhaps? That used to be quite popular, but it seems to have gone out of fashion lately. Nowadays, all the princes are talking birds, or dogs, or hedgehogs."

"No, no, I'm not in love with anyone!"

"Then what, exactly, is your problem?" the fairy said in exasperation.

"This!" Cimorene gestured at the castle around her. "Embroidery lessons, and dancing, and—and being a princess!"

"My dear Cimorene!" the fairy said, shocked. "It's your heritage!"

"It's boring."

"Boring?" The fairy did not appear to believe what she was hearing.

"Boring. I want to do things, not sit around all day and listen to the court minstrel make up songs about how brave Daddy is and how lovely his wife and daughters are."

"Nonsense, my dear. This is just a stage you're going through. You'll outgrow it soon, and you'll be very glad you didn't do anything rash."

Cimorene looked at her godmother suspiciously. "You've been talking to my parents, haven't you?"

"Well, they do try to keep me up-to-date on what my godchildren are doing."

"I thought so," said Cimorene, and bade her fairy godmother a polite good-bye.

A few weeks later, Cimorene's parents took her to a tourney in Sathem-by-the-Mountains, the next kingdom over. Cimorene was quite sure that the only reason they were taking her was because her fairy godmother had told them that something had better be done about Cimorene, and soon. She kept this opinion to herself; anything was better than the endless rounds of dancing and embroidery lessons at home.

Cimorene realized her mistake almost as soon as they reached their destination. For the king of Sathem-by-the-Mountains had a son, a golden-haired, blue-eyed, and exceedingly handsome prince, whose duties appeared to consist entirely of dancing attendance on Cimorene.

"*Isn't* he handsome," sighed Cimorene's lady-in-waiting.

"Yes," Cimorene said without enthusiasm. "Unfortunately, he isn't anything else."

"Whatever do you mean?" the lady-in-waiting said in astonishment.

"He has no sense of humor, he isn't intelligent, he can't talk about anything except tourneys, and half of what he does say he gets wrong. I'm glad we're only staying three weeks; I don't think I could stand to be polite to him for much longer than that."

"But what about your engagement?" the lady-in-waiting cried, horrified.

"What engagement?" Cimorene said sharply.

The lady-in-waiting tried to mutter something about a mistake, but Cimorene put up her chin in her best princess fashion and insisted on an explanation. Finally, the lady-in-waiting broke down.

"I . . . I overheard Their Majesties discussing it yesterday," she sniffled into her handkerchief. "The stipulations and covenants and contracts and settlements have all been drawn up, and they're going to sign them the day after tomorrow and announce it on Th-Thursday."

"I see," said Cimorene. "Thank you for telling me. You may go."

The lady-in-waiting left, and Cimorene went to see her parents. They were annoyed and a little embarrassed to find that Cimorene had discovered their plans, but they were still very firm about it. "We were going to tell you tomorrow, when we signed the papers," her father said.

"We knew you'd be pleased, dear," her mother said, nodding. "He's such a good-looking boy."

"But I don't want to marry Prince Therandil," Cimorene said.

"Well, it's not exactly a brilliant match," Cimorene's father said, frowning. "But I didn't think you'd care how big his kingdom was."

"It's the prince I don't care for," Cimorene said.

"That's a great pity, dear, but it can't be helped," Cimorene's mother said placidly. "I'm afraid it isn't likely that you'll get another offer."

"Then I won't get married at all."

Both her parents looked slightly shocked. "My dear Cimorene!" said her father. "That's out of the question. You're a princess; it simply isn't *done*."

"I'm too young to get married!"

"Your great-aunt Rose was married at sixteen," her mother pointed out. "One really can't count all those years she spent asleep under that dreadful fairy's curse."

"I won't marry the prince of Sathem-by-the-Mountains!" Cimorene said desperately. "It isn't proper!"

"What?" said both her parents together.

"He hasn't rescued me from a giant or an ogre, or freed me from a magic spell," Cimorene said.

Both her parents looked uncomfortable. "Well, no," said Cimorene's father. "It's a bit late to start arranging it, but we might be able to manage something."

"I don't think it's necessary," Cimorene's mother said. She looked reprovingly at Cimorene. "You've never paid attention to what was or wasn't suitable before, dear; you can't start now. Proper or not, you will marry Prince Therandil three weeks from Thursday."

"But, Mother—"

"I'll send the wardrobe mistress to your room to start fitting your bride clothes," Cimorene's mother said firmly, and that was the end of the conversation.

Cimorene decided to try a more direct approach: She went to see Prince Therandil. He was in the castle armory, looking at swords. "Good morning, Princess," he said, when he finally noticed Cimorene. "Don't you think this is a lovely sword?"

Cimorene picked it up. "The balance is off," she said.

"I believe you're right," said Therandil after a moment's study. "Pity; now I'll have to find another. Is there something I can do for you?"

"Yes," said Cimorene. "You can *not* marry me."

"What?" Therandil looked confused.

"You don't really want to marry me, do you?" Cimorene said coaxingly.

"Well, no," Therandil replied, looking sheepish.

"Oh, good. Then you'll tell your father you don't want to marry me?"

"I couldn't do that!" Therandil said, shocked. "It wouldn't be right."

"Why not?" Cimorene demanded crossly.

"Because . . . because . . . well, because princes just don't do that!"

"Then how are you going to keep from marrying me?"

"I guess I won't be able to," Therandil said, after thinking hard for a moment. "What do you think of that sword over there with the silver hilt?"

Cimorene left in disgust and went out to the castle garden. She was very discouraged; it looked as if she were going to have to marry the prince of Sathem-by-the-Mountains whether she wanted to or not. "I'd rather be eaten by a dragon," she muttered.

"That can be arranged," said a voice from beside her left slipper.

Cimorene looked down and saw a small, green frog looking up at her. "I beg your pardon; did you speak?" she asked.

"You don't see anyone else around, do you?" said the frog.

"Oh!" said Cimorene. She had never met a talking

frog before. "Are you an enchanted prince?" she asked a little doubtfully.

"No, but I've met a couple of them, and after a while you pick up a few things," said the frog. "Now, why is it that you want to be eaten by a dragon?"

"My parents want to marry me off to Prince Therandil," Cimorene explained.

"And you don't want to marry him? Sensible of you," said the frog. "I don't like Therandil; he used to skip rocks across the top of my pond. They always sank into my living room."

"I'm sorry," Cimorene said politely.

"Well," said the frog, "what are you going to do about it?"

"Marrying Therandil? I don't know. I've tried talking to my parents, but they won't listen, and neither will Therandil."

"I didn't ask what you'd said about it," the frog snapped. "I asked what you're going to do. Nine times out of ten, talking is a way of avoiding doing things."

"What kinds of things would you suggest?" Cimorene said, stung.

"You could challenge the prince to a duel," the frog said.

"He'd win," Cimorene said. "It's been four years since I've been allowed to do any fencing."

"You could turn him into a toad," the frog suggested.

"I never got past invisibility in my magic lessons," Cimorene said. "Transformations are advanced study."

The frog looked at her disapprovingly. "Can't you do anything?"

"I can curtsy," Cimorene said disgustedly. "I know seventeen different country dances, nine ways to agree with an ambassador from Cathay without actually promising him anything, and one hundred and forty-three embroidery stitches. And I can make cherries jubilee."

"Cherries jubilee?" asked the frog, and snapped at a passing fly.

"The castle chef taught me, before Father made him stop," Cimorene explained.

The frog munched briefly, then swallowed and said, "I suppose there's no help for it. You'll have to run away."

"Run away?" Cimorene said. "I don't like that idea; there are too many things that could go wrong."

"You don't like the idea of marrying Prince Therandil, either," the frog pointed out.

"Maybe I can think of some other way out of getting married."

The frog snorted. "Such as?" Cimorene didn't answer, and after a moment, the frog said, "I thought so. Do you want my advice or not?"

"Yes, please," said Cimorene. After all, she didn't have to follow it.

"Go to the main road outside the city and follow it away from the mountains," said the frog. "After a while, you will come to a small pavillion made of gold, surrounded by trees made of silver with emerald leaves.

Go straight past it without stopping, and don't answer if anyone calls out to you from the pavillion. Keep on until you reach a hovel. Walk straight up to the door and knock three times; then snap your fingers and go inside. You'll find some personages there who can help you out of your difficulties, if you're polite about asking and they're in the right mood. And that's all."

The frog turned abruptly and dove into the pool. "Thank you very much," Cimorene called after it, thinking that the frog's advice sounded very odd indeed. She went back into the castle.

Cimorene spent the rest of the day being fitted and fussed over by the ladies-in-waiting until she was ready to scream. By the end of the formal banquet, at which she had to sit next to Prince Therandil and listen to endless stories of his prowess in battle, Cimorene was more than ready to take the frog's advice.

Late that night, when most of the castle was asleep, Cimorene bundled up five clean handkerchiefs and her best crown. Then she dug out the notes she had taken during her magic lessons and carefully cast a spell of invisibility. It seemed to work, but she was still very careful about sneaking out of the castle. After all, it had been a long time since she had practiced.

By morning, Cimorene was well outside the city, and visible again, walking down the main road that led away from the mountains. It was hot and dusty, and she began to wish she had brought a bottle of water instead of the handkerchiefs.

Just before noon, Cimorene spied a small grove of

trees next to the road ahead of her. It looked like a cool, pleasant place to rest for a few minutes, and she hurried forward. When she reached the grove, however, she saw that the trees were made of the finest silver, and their shining green leaves were huge emeralds. In the center of the grove was a charming pavillion made of gold and hung with gold curtains.

Cimorene slowed down and looked longingly at the cool, green shade beneath the trees. Just then a woman's voice called out from the pavillion, "My dear, you look so tired and thirsty! Come and sit with me and share my luncheon."

The voice was so kind and coaxing that Cimorene took two steps toward the edge of the road before she remembered the frog's advice. "Oh, no," she thought to herself, "I'm not going to be caught this easily!" She turned without saying anything and hurried on down the road.

A little farther on, she came to a tiny, wretched-looking hovel made of cracked and weathered, grey boards. They door hung slantwise on a broken hinge, and the whole building looked as though it were going to topple over at any moment. Cimorene stopped and stared doubtfully at it, but she had followed the frog's advice this far and she thought it would be silly to stop now. So she shook the dust from her skirts and put on her crown (so as to make a good impression). She marched up to the door, knocked three times, and snapped her fingers just as the frog had told her. Then she pushed the door open and went inside.

The inside of the hovel was dark and cool and damp. Cimorene found it a pleasant relief after the hot, dusty road, but she wondered why no sunlight seemed to be coming through the cracks in the boards. She was still standing just inside the door, waiting for her eyes to adjust to the dark, when someone said crossly, "Is this that princess we've been waiting for?"

"Why don't you ask her?" said a deep, rumbly voice.

"I'm Cimorene, princess of Linderwall," Cimorene said, and tried to curtsy in the direction of the voices. "I was told you could help me."

"Help her?" said the first voice, and Cimorene heard a snort. "I think we should just eat her and be done with it."

Cimorene began to feel frightened. She felt behind her for the door, and started in surprise when her fingers touched damp stone instead of dry wood. Then a third voice said, "Not so fast, Woraug. Let's hear her story first."

So Cimorene took a deep breath and began to explain about the fencing lessons, and the magic lessons, and the Latin, and the juggling, and all the other things that weren't considered proper behavior for a princess, and she told the voices that she had run away from Sathem-by-the-Mountains to keep from having to marry Prince Therandil. "And what do you expect us to do about it?" one of the voices said curiously.

"I don't know," Cimorene said. "Except, of course, that I *would* rather not be eaten. I can't see who you are in this dark, you know."

"That can be fixed," said the voice. A moment later, a small ball of light appeared in the air above Cimorene's head. Cimorene stepped backward very quickly and ran into the wall. The voices belonged to dragons. Five of them lay on or sprawled over or curled around the various rocks and columns that filled the huge cave where Cimorene stood. She saw no sign of the hovel or the door through which she had entered.

Cimorene felt very frightened. The smallest of the dragons was easily three times as tall as she was, and they gave an overwhelming impression of shining, green scales and sharp, silver teeth. She swallowed very hard, wondering whether she really would rather be eaten by a dragon than marry Therandil.

"Well?" said the dragon just in front of her. "Just what are you asking us to do for you?"

"I—" Cimorene stopped short, as an idea occurred to her; then she asked cautiously, "Dragons are . . . are fond of princesses, aren't they?"

"Very," said the dragon, and smiled. The smile showed all of its teeth, which Cimorene did not find reassuring.

"That is, I've heard of dragons who have captive princesses to cook for them and . . . and so on," said Cimorene, who really had very little idea what captive princesses did all day.

The dragon in front of Cimorene nodded. One of the others, a yellowish-green in color, shifted restlessly and said, "Oh, let's just go ahead and eat her. It will save trouble."

Before any of the other dragons could answer, there

was a loud booming noise and a sixth dragon slithered into the cave. Its scales were more grey than green, and the dragons by the door made way for it respectfully. "Kazul!" said the newcomer in a loud voice. "*Achoo!* Sorry I'm late, but a terrible thing happened on the way here, *achoo!*"

"What was it?" said the dragon to whom Cimorene had been talking.

"Ran into a wizard. *Achoo!* Had to eat him; no help for it. *Achoo, achoo.* And now look at me!" Every time the grey-green dragon sneezed, he emitted a small ball of fire that scorched the wall of the cave.

"Calm down, Roxim," said Kazul. "You're only making it worse."

"*Achoo!* Calm down? When I'm having an allergy attack? *Achoo, oh, bother, achoo!*" said the grey-green dragon. "Somebody give me a handkerchief. *Achoo!*"

"Here," said Cimorene, holding out one of the ones she had brought with her. "Use this." She was beginning to feel much less frightened, for the grey-green dragon reminded her of her great-uncle, who was old and rather hard of hearing, and of whom she was rather fond.

"What's that?" said Roxim. "*Achoo!* Oh, hurry up and give it here."

Kazul took the handkerchief from Cimorene, using two claws very delicately, and passed it to Roxim. The grey-green dragon mopped his streaming eyes and blew his nose. "That's better, I think. *Achoo!* Oh, drat!"

The ball of fire that accompanied the dragon's sneeze

had reduced the handkerchief to a charred scrap. Cimorene hastily dug out another one and handed it to Kazul, feeling very glad that she had brought several spares.

Roxim went through two more handkerchiefs before his sneezing spasms finally stopped. "Much better," he said. "Now then, who's this that lent me the handkerchiefs? Somebody's new princess, eh?"

"We were just discussing that when you came in," Kazul said, and turned back to Cimorene. "You were saying? About cooking and so on."

"Couldn't I do that for one of you for a while?" Cimorene said.

The dragon smiled again, and Cimorene swallowed hard. "Possibly. Why would you want to do that?"

"Because then I wouldn't have to go home and marry Therandil," Cimorene said. "Being a dragon's princess is a perfectly respectable thing to do, so my parents couldn't complain. And it would be much more interesting than embroidery and dancing lessons."

Several of the dragons made snorting or choking noises. Cimorene jumped, then decided that they were laughing.

"This is ridiculous!" said a large, bright-green dragon on Cimorene's left.

"Why?" asked Kazul.

"A princess, volunteering? Out of the question!"

"That's easy for you to say," one of the other dragons grumbled. "You already have a princess. What about the rest of us?"

"Yes, don't be stuffy, Woraug," said another. "Besides, what else can we do with her?"

"Eat her," suggested the yellowish-green dragon in a bored tone.

"No proper princess would come out looking for dragons," Woraug objected.

"Well, I'm not a proper princess, then," Cimorene snapped. "I make cherries jubilee, and I volunteer for dragons, and I conjugate Latin verbs—or at least, I would if anyone would let me. So there!"

"Hear, hear," said the grey-green dragon.

"You see?" Woraug said. "Who would want an improper princess?"

"I would," said Kazul.

"Give her a trial run first," a purplish-green dragon advised.

"You can't be serious, Kazul," Woraug said irritably. "Why?"

"I like cherries jubilee," Kazul replied, still watching Cimorene. "And I like the look of her. Besides, the Latin scrolls in my library need cataloging, and if I can't find someone who knows a little of the language, I'll have to do it myself."

"And for that you'd take on a black-haired, snippy, little—"

"I'll thank you to be polite when you're discussing *my* princess," Kazul said, and smiled fiercely.

"Nice little gal," Roxim said, nodding approvingly and waving Cimorene's next-to-last handkerchief. "Got sense. Be good for you, Kazul."

"If that's settled, I'm going to go find a snack," said the yellowish-green dragon.

Woraug looked around, but the other dragons seemed to agree with Roxim. "Oh, very well," Woraug said grumpily. "It's your choice after all, Kazul."

"It certainly is. Now, Princess, if you'll come this way, I'll get you settled in."

Cimorene followed Kazul across the cave and down a tunnel. She was relieved to find that the ball of light came with her; she had the uncomfortable feeling that if she had tried to walk behind a dragon in the dark she would have stepped on its tail, which would not have been a good beginning.

Kazul led Cimorene through a long maze of tunnels and finally stopped in another chamber. "Here we are," the dragon said. "You can use the small room over on the right; I believe my last princess left most of the furnishings behind when she ran off with the knight."

"Thank you," Cimorene said. "When do I start my duties? And what are they, please?"

"You start right away," said Kazul. "I'll want dinner at seven. In the meantime you can start sorting the treasure." The dragon nodded toward a dark opening on the left. "I'm sure some of it needs repairing; there's at least one suit of armor with the leg off, and some of the cheaper magic swords are probably getting rusty. The rest of it really ought to be rearranged sensibly. I can never find anything when I want it."

"What about the library you mentioned?" Cimorene said.

"We'll see how well you do on the treasure room first," Kazul said. "The rest of your job I'll explain as we go along. You don't object to learning a little magic, do you?"

"Not at all," said Cimorene.

"Good. It'll make things much easier. Go and wash up a little, and I'll let you into the treasure room so you can get started."

Cimorene nodded and went to the room Kazul had told her to use. As she washed her face and hands, she felt happier than she had in a long time. She was not going to have to marry Therandil, and sorting a dragon's treasure sounded far more interesting than dancing or embroidery. She was even going to learn some magic! For the first time in her life, Cimorene was glad she was a princess. She dried her hands and turned to go back into the main chamber, wondering how best to persuade Kazul to help her brush up on her Latin. She didn't want the dragon to be disappointed in her skill. *"Draco, draconis, draconi,"* she muttered, and her lips curved into a smile. She had always been rather good at declining nouns. Still smiling, she started forward to begin her new duties.

Watch Out!

by Bruce Coville

"I'm home!" yelled Kirby Markle, bursting through the front door of his house. Without waiting for an answer, he pounded up the stairs and dashed into his bedroom. Flopping down onto his bed, he tore open the box he had bought at that strange store he found when he took the new shortcut home.

Inside he found a second box. "THE CAVE OF THE GNOME," proclaimed bold, black letters written across the top.

Underneath, in smaller print, it said, "Fool Your Family! Amaze Your Friends! A Fascinating Device for Both Amateur and Professional Magicians."

Kirby examined the box with wide eyes. Maybe this would finally be the trick he got to work. The old man who had sold it to him said it was especially good for someone like him, who was in a hurry to learn magic.

Fumbling with the tape that held the box shut, Kirby tore open the flaps and held the box upside down over his bed.

Out tumbled a cave made of papier-mâché.

A look of uncertainty crossed Kirby's face. He couldn't see any way that this was going to make things disappear.

"Kirby! Supper!"

Kirby sighed. He really didn't want to go to supper now. He wanted to figure out how to make this trick work.

"Just a minute, Mom!"

He began reading the directions.

"Kirby!"

"All right, all right. I'm coming!" Kirby shoved the directions into his pocket and bolted down the stairs.

As soon as supper was over, Kirby asked his mother and father to come into the living room. "I have something I want to show you," he said.

He herded them through the door and onto the couch, then raced back upstairs to grab the cave.

"I got a new trick today," he announced, as he hurtled back down the steps, two and three at a time.

Kirby's parents exchanged smiles. Kirby wanted so badly to be a magician. But he had never yet gotten a trick to work properly. He was always so eager to show them off that he never took the time to learn how to do them right.

"Did you read the directions yet?" asked his mother.

"Sort of," said Kirby. "It's gonna be great. Now, I need something to put in the cave. Can I have your watch, Dad?"

Kirby's father looked properly doubtful. "Will I get it back?" he asked.

"Oh, Dad."

"Well, okay," said his father, smiling. "But be careful with it. It's quite expensive."

He took out his pocket watch and gave it to Kirby.

"Now, watch this," said Kirby. He put the watch in the cave. Then he rolled the little papier-mâché boulder across the front of it. Putting his right hand on the cave he read the magic words off the instruction sheet, at the same time giving the top a little twist to the right. He smiled to himself. The twist must be what activated the mechanism that would hide the watch.

BOOM!

The noise was so loud it actually shook the windows. A puff of smoke rose from the cave, and red flames licked out around the little boulder.

Kirby snatched his hand away. "Ow!" he cried.

Mr. and Mrs. Markle looked at each other nervously.

Trying to act casual, Kirby removed the boulder from the front of the cave.

The watch was gone.

"Presto kazam!" he said with a big smile. "A genuine magic trick!"

Kirby's parents applauded dutifully. But his father

had a worried look on his face. "Why don't you bring it back now?" he said gently.

"You bet!" said Kirby. He put the boulder back in front of the cave and twisted the top to the left.

Nothing happened.

He tried it again.

Nothing happened.

He twisted it to the right.

Nothing happened.

Kirby snatched up the directions and began reading frantically through them. Suddenly he turned very pale.

"What is it, Kirby?" asked his mother.

Without saying a word, Kirby handed her the paper.

* * *

Gregory Gnome was puttering about in his cave when he heard the bell ring. A greedy smile crossed his face, and he ran to the loading platform.

The smile faded a little. Another gold watch. Well, it was better than a kick in the pants, he thought with a shrug. Taking the watch to the storage area, he tossed it into a box already close to overflowing with watches. He really would have to have a cave sale someday soon to turn some of this junk into usable cash.

"Gregory!" said a voice behind him. "Aren't you ashamed of yourself, taking advantage of all those children?"

Gregory winced. His face took on an injured expression. As he turned to his wife, he pulled a sheet of paper from his pocket. "Look at these directions," he said. "Read the last paragraph to me."

It was his wife's turn to sigh. "I don't have to read it," she said. "I know it by heart: 'Once an object is placed in the Cave of the Gnome, it can never be returned. So please be sure to use only objects that have no real value.'"

"Well, there it is," said Gregory, looking soulful. "It could hardly be any plainer, could it? All I wanted to do was give kids a toy they could have some fun with. Can I help it if not one out of twenty is smart enough to read the directions before he tries to use the thing? Can I?"

No matter how hard he tried to look serious, Gregory could not hide the greedy smile that twitched at the corners of his mouth.

* * *

The little papier-mâché cave was in tiny pieces all over Kirby's living-room floor.

Of papier mâché there was a lot. Of the gold watch, not a trace.

"Kirby," said Mr. Markle, "come with me. I want to have a little talk with you."

Slowly, very slowly, Kirby followed his father out of the room.

The Silver Leopard

by Robert Lawson

There were often told in the foothills of Karm tales of
a strange sort of leopard. Once perhaps in every gen-
eration some wild hillsman coming down to the valley
villages would bring word of one having been seen.

Then would the old wives, gathered about the fire
of an evening, spin long and reminiscent stories of
former reports of this sort. They would tell of the mad
hillsman who had appeared during the winter of the
black snows claiming to have seen one of these silver
leopards. Women he claimed they were (but then he
was mad), of the size and shape of an ordinary leopard,
and all covered with tiny scales of silver so that they
shone in the sun like a new, polished breastplate. The
one he had seen had passed him by, all unconscious
apparently of his presence, and he, smitten by some
strange attraction, had followed her for many days.
She had not seemed to hasten or to attempt flight, yet

try as he would he could not overtake her—until finally the madness had come upon him and he had fled to the foothills.

Return to the mountains he would not, but he remained for many years in the valleys, telling to all who would listen of the fierce power of attraction wielded by "her of the silver scales," and warning the youths of the villages to beware of it. That his words had the usual result of such warnings was proved by the fact that after the coming of each rumor many young hunters turned their footsteps toward the hills. That his fears seemed well founded was borne out by the old women's tales, always ending as they did with that monotonous and sinister phrase, "they never came back."

Differing in many minor points, these tales all seemed to agree at least in their description of the little-seen beasts. That they walked always alone, scornful and indifferent of both man and beast alike. Cold and glistening, unapproachable and unsullied, they pursued their solitary ways. Of their origin or ways of life— what they hunted, where they lived—none knew. That they never mated seemed certain, for what male, even the greatest and whitest of the snow leopards of the North, had the temerity to dream of running the hills beside one of these gleaming beings?

Neither could anyone explain their fateful fascination for men. Some said that it was the value of their pelts, some that it was the desire of the hunters to accomplish that wherein all others had failed, that lured them to an unknown fate.

It is but natural that such tales, heard since childhood, should have fired the imagination of Marik, youngest and boldest of all the hunters of the Ten Valleys. Often in his long and lonely hunts he had pondered on the ways of these rare beasts, and he had resolved that the day upon which he attained the age of manhood should see the beginning of his greatest and most perilous hunt.

So it was that on an evening in late summer Marik stole softly from the house of his father and turned toward the Mountains of Karm. Wrapped in his cloak was the Flute of the River Waters, and his quiver held the Seven Ancestral Arrows.

Last reports had it that a silver leopard was to be found in the vicinity of the Black Hill, which was in the southern part of the mountains. Here then Marik betook himself, and day after day made music strange indeed to those lonely places.

He played of the Northern Rivers, a wild and turbulent song filled with the scream of the eagles and the crashing of ice upon stones. He played of the rivers of East and West, broad bosomed and strong, and the volume of sound woke the deer in the far-off Malian Meadows.

Then one day as he played the languorous song of the Warmer Waters, there came into his sight a creature such as even he, who had seen much that others had not, had never even dreamed. A leopard, greater than any of the tribe, yet so supple and of such grace that she seemed to have no weight but glided on like the winter lights, wrapped in the cold radiance of her silver coat. Proud headed and superb she passed across the slope. Her eyes, pale and flickering, surveyed him with no more interest than had he been one of the rocks which dotted the hillside. So without pause, without haste, she passed.

Wild then grew the music. All the heat and passion of the Southern Waters rose like the noon wind of the desert, yet she tarried not nor turned her head.

Then indeed did Marik know that it was beyond the power of music to subdue such a one and that he must turn to the chase. Throwing aside the flute, he slung about his waist the quiver containing the arrows of his ancestors, and bow in hand followed the spot of radiance that now shimmered far off among the trees.

Of the chase that followed it were but monotony to relate, for each day was but the same, and like each day was each month. The months dragged into a year, and still was Marik no closer to his quarry.

Six of his arrows had he drawn to the head and six times had the mighty bow begun its song of death, that song that ends with the cry of the smitten. Yet six arrows were shattered on the rocks, and the song unfinished. Many times he thought that the madness had come upon him and that it was but a distant phantom that lured him on. Always the supple movement and radiant purity of that silver form lit his brain, and greater grew the desire to grasp that rounded throat, to see the blood, rich and warm, well up from beneath its cold covering: To hear the breath break its even beat and gush in great sobs; to alter the unchanging, green stare of those icelike eyes; to see in them terror or hate—or love.

Long had the Southern Hills been left behind, and they now wandered in the cold Northern Mountains of Karm. To Marik was now left but the Arrow of the Seventh Ancestor, that very arrow which, launched at the moon, had remained in the air nine days and nine nights. Of all arrows fashioned by the hand of man this was the greatest, and it he had saved for the last.

Then one day, near the great, red peak of Karmara, beyond which there is snow and men know not, Marik knew that that day must be the last.

And on that day he saw her, plain and clear to view, coming toward him across a small valley.

Fitting to his bowstring the last arrow and murmuring a prayer to that great ancestor who had fashioned it, he drew to the full and released. Straight and full to the mark the arrow flew, and as it sank deep in the throat of the silver leopard, she sprang high in the air. Loud among the icy hills sang the death song of the great bow, clear to its shrill ending.

As the leopard, shining like a falling comet, dropped to the earth, the silver scales shook from her body as blossoms from a stricken tree. And the form that they had covered was but the form of an ordinary leopard—

neither more beautiful nor more desirable than that of any of the common tribes that roam the valleys.

As he looked upon the sight there came upon the heart of Marik a great weariness and longing for the peace and rest of the valleys. Sadly gathering the splintered remnants of the last arrow, he spurned the body of the great, dead cat with his foot, and he returned to his native place.

When he told the people there of his hunt and of its ending, they laughed at him in scorn, saying that he had failed and had become mad.

"For," they said, "he would have at least brought home the silver scales and with them bought a farm."

* * *

And still do the youngest and boldest of the valley hunters turn their footsteps toward the hills to hunt that glittering vision whose radiance blinds them to all else. Whether the madness comes upon them or whether they succeed—and if succeeding, they are content with that which they have secured—the old wives cannot say. For the quiet valleys slumbering in the sun know them no more.

Truce

by Anne Eliot Crompton

Mayday at sunrise, my mother came to Girls' House.

She brought me a pouch of parched corn and a small, white stone. She said, "On my Mayday I carried this stone." She dropped it in with the corn and tied the pouch to my belt.

My mother kissed me. For years I had not felt the warmth of her arms, and now I might not feel it again. Not every girl returns from her Mayday.

My best friend kissed me. Her cheek was tear damp. Quickly, before dread could seize me, I set the dagger into my belt and left Girls' House.

Mist rose from the circling forest. I strode past Long House and Slave House and out through the gardens. I passed bowed man-slaves hilling earth, sisters and mothers scraping seed corn. With all my heart I wished I carried a seed basket and hoe, and not this dagger!

If only I could work and joke and swim with the sisters today!

Carefully, no one spoke to me. I spoke to no one. I entered our forest.

Mist rose from moist earth and curled among new leaves. Giantess trees stood with their children about their knees. The trail wound among bushes, some good for fruit, some for fabric. Our forest is also our garden.

I knew every step of our forest, every trail, cliff and cave. I knew where to find animals and where they might find me. I knew the track and sign of every creature except the one I sought that morning.

This quarry leaves no track, no sign. You may meet him on a cliff top or in a ravine, thicket or clearing. You meet him once, when and where you are ready.

Softly trotting the trail, I wondered. Was I ready? My body told me so. The sisters told me so, praising my height and skills. The mothers told me so, sending me out alone this Mayday. I should be ready to meet White One.

I was ready enough to meet anything else. Hah! I knew the uses of a dagger, also of hands and teeth. We have small bears in our forest, and bad-tempered hogs. Truly dangerous are the dog packs that sometimes cross our stone borders. But when their fierce voices are heard, the foresters hasten to hunt them away. My danger of meeting dogs was slight.

The thought of dogs weakened me, however, so I pushed it away. That which you think of you draw toward you. Resolutely, I thought of White One.

Every girl has heard of him, though his story is not told in Long House of a winter night. No one speaks of him aloud. But mothers whisper of him to small daughters. Girls bathing in the river murmur of him, softer than flowing water.

They say he looks like a moon-white buck, one-horned. The horn juts, long and ribbed, from his forehead. They say his eyes glow red. They say you cannot hunt him out, he comes to you. As you sit waiting alone in the Mayday forest he comes to you, and lays his head in your lap. You rise up then, woman-grown.

When you come home, no one asks if you have met White One. That is your secret. Your mother, your best friend, will not ask. But they will know by your bearing, by your step and by your eyes.

Thinking of this I paused on the trail to pray. I touched the white stone in my pouch and whispered, "White One, I am ready. Come to me."

At noon I reached my chosen cliff. Others had chosen it before me. The rock is pocked with finger and toe holes chiseled long ago and worn smooth by hundreds of climbing girls. Halfway up the cliff is a ledge. Here, in the strong spring sun, overlooking our lands, I meant to wait for the White One.

I had climbed these holes before, when I was smaller and lighter. Crawling onto the sun-baked ledge this time I found myself panting. I sat up cross-legged, back to the rock wall, and looked down on our lands.

Forest stretched everywhere. Northward, two hills marked our boundary. A pass led between the hills.

Here, the Grandmothers raised two standing stones, great black boulders. From the ledge I could not see those stones, but I knew their place. From the ledge I could not see the hundred trails that wound through our forest, but I knew each one like the lines of my palm. I did see the slow, shimmering river and the roofs of our village.

I heard deep, yapping voices far away. Dogs? Shivering in the sun, I touched my dagger.

The voices died away. The heat strengthened. I may have dozed.

If so, I woke sharply. I was still alone. White One had not come to my ledge. Touching the white stone in my pouch, I prayed silently, "White One, I am ready. I wait. Come to me."

Down below, under the cliff, something moved.

They say White One moves silently as moonlight. This something crashed about like a bear, breaking branches and pushing through thickets. I heard teeth tearing up grasses. Puzzled, I leaned over, looked down.

Never had I seen or heard of this creature. Large as a forester's grass hut, he was covered with short, red hair. A mane of long, black hair grew down his neck, and he whisked a tail of long, black hair. Stepping heavily on huge, round hoofs, he shook his mane, swished his tail, and snorted grandly.

First thought: Enough meat here to feed the village for a moon!

Second thought: Not much I can do about that, alone with my dagger.

Third thought: I am holding my stone. I just prayed. This red creature may be my guide, sent me by White One!

My breath came short with excitement. Red grabbed grass from the cliff's foot, looked around, snorted again, shouldered his way under the trees. I still caught glimpses of red and black through the leaves and heard the thud of hoofs.

Letting go the white stone, I scrambled down the cliff and sneaked along Red's broad, bruised trail.

Red stamped carelessly along the cliffside, snatching bites and snorting. I crept so close after him that once his black tail swept my face.

Ahead, a whistle.

Someone whistled as the foresters whistle to signal each other. Red moved faster, toward the sound.

Whishing tail toward me, Red ambled up to a person sitting under the cliff. Red bent his head, and the person somehow took hold of him and tried to climb him. She was injured. She tried to stand up with Red's help, but he backed away.

She must have fallen off the cliff. She had a shock of sunny hair and strange clothes. She was not one of Us. She saw me, and said, "Help me!" Her voice was deep and harsh. She was a man!

Or boy. Not much older than me. Beard like newborn cub's fur.

"Help me?"

I touched my dagger, my only weapon. He also carried only a dagger, which he did not touch.

This was my test! White One sent Red to lead me to this man. If I could capture him, mine would be the finest Mayday return ever made!

But to get at him I must pass Red, massively in the way.

Red must be on my side. White One sent him.

Cautiously I edged forward. Red looked around at me with dark, innocent eyes. Animal eyes. Around his head he had a rope that dangled down. His smell was pungent.

I came to the man/boy. He smiled up at me. His eyes were blue, his smile friendly. I stood over him, and still he did not move to defend himself.

He said, "I fell off the cliff."

"So I guessed." But how badly hurt was he? Hurt turned his freckles pale, but I thought he could still fight.

"I wrenched my ankle."

Was that all! Careful now, I thought. Slowly. Deception before force.

"My horse ran away, and that was just as well. A band of hunting Amazons rushed right past me, after him. Those women are monsters!"

Ha! The foresters were out, probably hunting the dogs I heard from the cliff.

"Girl," said the boy, "can you help me? If those hellish Amazons come back, I'm done for."

And I would lose the glory of his capture.

I said, "There is a cave yonder."

I got him to his feet and let him lean on me, hard

arm over my shoulders. He hobbled painfully, but I could feel his strength returning as we went. Alarming strength. He whistled like a forester, and Red followed us. This worried me. Red's trail was like a village path. Let the foresters not come near till I had secured my prize!

The cave was only a few paces away, hidden in thickets. Once inside, the boy relaxed. He seemed to have not even the faintest suspicion of me.

The cave was tall and narrow. To my surprise, Red came in with us. He did not sit down with us, however. He stood looking out over the bushes, nodding his head and muttering.

The boy and I sat together and talked. As we talked, the magic hours of Mayday passed.

His name was Ron. I told him I was Ria. Too late I remembered I should not tell my true name to a stranger, let alone an enemy! This was my first time talking with a stranger.

We whispered, because the foresters move like shadows and might be anywhere. We shared my parched corn. Ron had nothing in his pouch. "I am on quest," he said, "to become a man." And he blushed. He added, "We quest with one dagger, one horse, and an empty pouch."

Hah! So men, too, go on quest! And for what, I asked, did Ron quest?

I had had two surprises that Mayday. Red and Ron were surprises enough, I thought. But now I had a third surprise, an astonishment, like a blow. Ron

quested after White One! Like me, with this difference: that Ron meant to kill White One. Whom he
called Unicorn.

The double shock took my breath right away. But
even before I could speak again, I saw my chance.
Recovering, I whispered, "Ron, I also seek . . .
Unicorn."

Ron looked as shocked as I felt. "You? A girl?"

"We seek him as you do." Ron shook his head, un-
believing. "But not to kill. That is not thinkable." I
explained what White One meant to us, how he dealt
with us. I said, "If you promise not to attack White
One, I will help you find him."

I meant to lead Ron straight into the village.

Gloating, I convinced him to follow me, by moonlight, to White One's haunt.

My Mayday passed as we laid our plans, I keeping
my eyes lowered lest he glimpse treachery. If I was
mistaken, if Ron was not to be my prize, the magic
day was wasted.

Yet, sharing the last of the corn, I felt uneasy. We
had talked and eaten and exchanged names. Ron thought
I was his friend. He was surprisingly human, even
though he had a magic companion.

I asked about Red. "Is he magic?"

Ron laughed. "Red is my servant . . . and my friend."

"Magic?"

"No, Ria. Red is an animal."

I glanced up at Red, looming over us. His kind eyes

were animal. His smell was animal. Earlier, he had dumped a large pile of manure on the cave floor.

Ron said, "I ride him."

He went on to explain this "riding," but I hardly heard his words. I was listening to another sound, not far off, coming fast.

Ron said, "You've gone all white. What's wrong?"

"Dogs!"

He listened. "Yes, nearby." What calm!

"They are on our trail! Ron, dogs hunt by scent!"

"Hunt? You mean these are wild dogs?" Ron turned pale. "We'd best get out of here before they trap us." Shakily, Ron raised himself and grabbed Red's rope. With one hand he seized Red's coarse, black mane. He heaved himself up on Red's back!

Red pawed at the cave floor and stepped about, swishing his tail. His eyes showed white. His fear convinced me that he really was animal.

Sitting on Red's back, Ron commanded his strength and speed. In a moment they would be gone, leaving me to the dogs, who bayed nearer every moment.

Ron held out a hand to me. "Come *on*, Ria!"

I grabbed the hand. He hauled me up Red's mountainous side behind him. "Hold my waist." I wrapped my arms around Ron. "Hold on." I clamped my legs tight, like his.

The next instant Red tore out of the cave, through the bushes, away. I shut my eyes and hung on. Red bounded rhythmically; I caught on to the rhythm and moved with it. Cracking an eye, I saw earth running away below, and bushes, and a fallen branch, which we leaped, and a huge, black dog snapping at my heel.

Heel *up*, eyes *shut*. We bowed low, low to Red's side, under swishing branches. The booming dog voices fell away behind us.

Red moved slower, rhythm broken. Cheek to Ron's shoulder I opened my eyes and saw the Bear Tree jog past, and knew what trail we traveled.

Red slowed to a bone-shifting walk. Ron straightened up, relaxed. I murmured, "Ron. I'm not going past the standing stones."

Ron jerked, surprised, and Red stopped. Ron shuddered. "You are one of Them?" Horror shook his body.

I said, "I am an Amazon, as you are a man."

Birds sang. Red snorted. I hung on to Ron's waist.

He said slowly, "You are not a true Amazon yet, Ria, as I am not yet a man." He would have said more, but I shushed him, squeezing his waist.

"Listen!"

Ron whispered, "Bird calls."

"That whistle. That's a forester's. They are on Red's track." And no track could be easier to follow!

I slipped down Red's warm side to stand in the trail. "Ron, ride to the standing stones. Beyond, you are safe. I will turn the foresters here."

"But . . ." Pale with fear, Ron hesitated. For me.

"They are my folk, Ron."

He nodded, and touched Red with his heel. They jogged away.

I hoped to train as a forester. I wanted to run these trails, hunt dogs and men, count game, with the women who now appeared out of evening light. I knew them, each by name, before Ron's eye would even have noticed them. Slyly they came, spear-bristling, green-haired, green-skinned, their green clothes blood splotched. At sight of me they paused. They knew this was my Mayday. They would not speak or come too near.

They consulted together in their sign language. Then they said loudly, all together, "I smell man on this trail!" So I was warned. The foresters melted away, vanishing into twilight. Ron would have said they vanished like spirits, but I saw each one, how she moved. I followed the trail.

As I came in sight of the great standing stones, Ron stepped out before me. Red grazed nearby. Beyond him the stones reared, with mist between. And in the mist, a white shape. Eyes glowed.

I touched Ron's arm, signaling silence.

I lifted the white stone from my pouch and held it, warmed it, in my palm. I went a little way forward and sank down, cross-legged. "White One," I said, "I am ready. I wait. Come to me."

Head high, White One watched us.

Then slowly, daintily, he came. Delicate as a doe. Quietly he folded down beside me, and his small head, one-horned, came to rest on my knee.

He had no weight or smell. Gently, his eyes met mine. His horn grazed my cheek.

I was aware that Ron sat down beside me. His large hand touched the ribbed horn and drew back.

We three sat together as darkness closed in. We heard Red nearby, plucking grass with his blunt teeth, stepping with heavy hoofs. The birds fell silent, and the moon rose.

White One raised his head. His eyes flashed red as he stood up. A moment he looked down on us, then he turned away, pranced three steps in the moonlight, and vanished.

I stood up a woman.

Ron stood up a man. He said, "Ria, come with me."

"Not past those stones."

"Meet me here, next Mayday."

"I will do that."

Ron pressed my hands in his big, warm ones. I still look forward to next Mayday! Barely limping, he walked to Red, grasped his mane, and mounted. Raising a hand to me, he rode into the mist, between the standing stones.

I dropped the white stone into my pouch and turned homeward. Back there no one would ask if I had met White One. My mother, my best friend, would not ask. But they would know by my bearing, by my step, and by my eyes.

The Fable of the Three Princes

by Isaac Asimov

There was a king once named Hilderic who ruled over a very small kingdom known as Micrometrica. It was not a rich kingdom or a powerful one, but it was a happy one, because Hilderic was a good sort of king who loved his people and was loved by them.

Because Micrometrica was so small and poor, Hilderic did not try to conquer other kingdoms, and because it was so small and poor other kingdoms did not think it worthwhile to conquer it. As a result, all was peaceful and pleasant in Micrometrica.

Of course, King Hilderic didn't like to be poor. The palace was quite small, and he had to help in the garden while his wife, Queen Ermentrude, had to help in the kitchen. This made them both unhappy, but they did have an ample supply of one thing—sons.

One day, it so happened, the queen had had a child for the first time. All the kingdom would have been extremely happy, except that she overdid it. She had triplets. Three boys.

"Dear, dear," said King Hilderic, thoughtfully. "With triplets, how will we ever decide which one shall succeed to the throne?"

"Perhaps," said Queen Ermentrude, who looked at the three new babies with love and pride, "we can allow all three to rule when the time comes."

But King Hilderic shook his head. "I don't think so, my love. The kingdom is scarcely large enough for one ruler. All the other kingdoms will laugh if it has three. Besides, what if the three should disagree? Our people would be so unhappy with quarreling monarchs."

"Well," said the queen, "we'll decide when they grow up."

* * *

The three babies grew up tall and strong and handsome, and the royal parents loved them all equally. They saw to it that all three boys studied hard, so that each one might be perfectly fit to be a king when the time came.

Though all did very well in their studies, it soon became clear that the sons were not identical triplets. Their appearances and tastes were different.

One of the three princes was larger and stronger than either of the other two. He came to be called "Primus," which, in the ancient, sacred language of the kingdom, meant "number one."

When he was not at his studies, Prince Primus exercised and developed his muscles. He could lift heavy weights, bend thick iron bars, and crack a coconut in his bare hands.

Everyone in the kingdom admired his strength and thought they would feel safe if only he were the king when the time came for it.

Another son was not quite as tall or as strong as Prince Primus, and so he came to be called "Secundus," which, in that same ancient, sacred language meant "number two."

His muscles didn't bulge as those of Prince Primus did, but when he was not at his studies, he practiced with weapons of war. Prince Secundus could throw his spear farther and shoot an arrow straighter than anyone in the kingdom. No one could stand against him in a sword fight, and he rode a horse to perfection.

Everyone in the kingdom admired his skill and thought they would feel safe if he were the king, too.

The remaining son was reasonably tall and strong, but he was not quite as tall and strong as his two brothers, so he was named "Tertius," which meant "number three."

Prince Tertius was even better at his studies than his two brothers, but he was not interested in lifting weights or throwing spears. When he was not studying, he wrote love poems and would sing them in a very pleasant voice. He also read a great many books.

The young ladies of the kingdom thought the poetry of Prince Tertius was beautiful. Everyone else, however, wasn't sure it would be safe to have a poet as king. They were glad there were two stronger princes to choose from.

The three princes were quite friendly with each other, fortunately, and as they grew older, they decided that they would not fight or quarrel over who was to be the king someday. In fact, they loved their father and wanted him to stay king for many years.

"Still," said Prince Primus, "Our Royal Father is getting old, and we must come to some decision. Since we are all the same age there's no use trying to select the oldest. However, I am the largest and strongest. There's that to consider."

"Yes," said Prince Secundus, "but I am the most skilled warrior. I don't want to make a fuss about that, but it is important."

"I think," said Prince Tertius, "we ought to let Dad and Mom make the decision."

Prince Primus frowned. "I don't think you ought to call Our Royal Parents 'Dad and Mom.' "

"But that's who they are," said Prince Tertius.

"That is not the point," said Prince Secundus. "There is their dignity to think of. If I were king someday, I should certainly expect you to refer to me as 'My Royal Brother.' I should be very hurt if you were to call me 'buddy' or 'pal.' "

"That is very true," said Prince Primus. "If I were king, I would despise being called 'Primey.' "

"In that case," said Tertius, who never liked to quarrel, "why don't we ask Our Royal Parents what we ought to do? After all, they are the monarchs, and we should obey their wishes."

"Very well," said the other two, and all three rushed to the royal throne room.

* * *

King Hilderic thought about it. Being a good king, he wanted to do what was best for his little country. He wasn't at all sure that the country would be well off under a very strong king, or a very warlike king, or even a very poetic king.

What the country needed, he thought, was a very *rich* king, one who could spend money to make the country happier and more prosperous.

Finally, he sighed, and said, "There's no way I can choose among you. I will have to send you on a hard and dangerous quest to get money—a great deal of money. I don't want to make it seem that money is so terribly important, but, you know, we *do* need it quite badly. Therefore the one who brings back the most money will be king."

Queen Ermentrude looked very disturbed. "But, Father—" (She never called him "Your Majesty" unless courtiers were about, and the kingdom was so poor there weren't many of those.) "But, Father," she said, "what if our dear princes should be hurt in the course of the quest?"

"We can only hope they won't be hurt, Mother, but we need money you see, and Emperor Maximian of Allemania has a great deal of money. He is probably the richest monarch in the world."

Prince Primus said, "That may be so, My Royal Father, but the emperor won't give us money just because we ask for it."

Prince Secundus said, "In fact, no one will give us money just because we ask for it."

Prince Tertius said, "I don't think princes ought to ask for money in any case."

"Well, my princes," said the King, "it is not a matter of asking for money. The emperor Maximian, it seems, has a daughter named Meliversa. She is an only child."

He put on a large pair of spectacles and pulled a stiff sheet of parchment from a drawer in the royal desk.

He said, "I received this notice by courier two days ago, and I have been studying it ever since. It has been distributed to all the kings in the world, and it is really very kind of the emperor to remember me, since I am king of so small and poor a country."

He cleared his throat. "It says here," he said, glancing over the parchment very carefully, "that the imperial princess is as beautiful as the day; tall, slender, and very well educated."

Prince Primus said, "It's a little troublesome to have a princess well educated. She may talk too much."

"But we needn't listen to her," said Prince Secundus.

Prince Tertius said, "But My Royal Father, what has the imperial princess got to do with the matter of obtaining money?"

"Well, my young princes," said the King, "anyone who is a royal prince, and who can prove he is one by presenting his birth certificate, will be allowed to demonstrate his abilities. If these should please the imperial princess Meliversa so that she wishes to marry the prince, he will be named successor to the throne and given a large allowance. Then, eventually, he will become emperor. If it is one of you, why then he will also become king of this country in time; and with the wealth of the empire to dispose of, he will make Micrometrica very prosperous."

Prince Primus said, "The princess Meliversa could never resist my muscles, My Royal Father."

Prince Secundus said, "Or my horsemanship, if it comes to that."

Prince Tertius said, "I wonder if she likes poetry. . . ."

King Hilderic said, "There is one catch though. I have educated you boys in economics, sociology, and other subjects a king must know. Meliversa, however, has been educated in sorcery. If any prince tries to win her heart and fails, she will turn him into a statue. She says she needs a great many statues for the promenade in her park."

Queen Ermentrude said, "I knew it," and began to weep.

"Don't weep, My Royal Mother," said Prince Tertius, who loved her dearly. "I'm sure it isn't legal to turn princes into statues."

"Not ordinarily." said the king, "but it is part of the agreement. Besides, it is difficult to argue law with an imperial princess. So if you princes don't want to take the chance, I certainly won't blame you. . . . It's just that we need money so badly."

Prince Primus said, "I am not afraid. She will never be able to resist me."

"Or me," said Prince Secundus.

Prince Tertius looked thoughtful and said nothing.

*　*　*

The three princes made ready at once for the long journey. Their clothing was rather faded and out of fashion, and their horses were old, but that was all they could manage.

"Farewell, My Royal Parents," said Prince Primus. "I shall not fail you."

"I hope not," said King Hilderic doubtfully, while Queen Ermentrude wept quietly in the background.

"I shall not fail you either, My Royal Parents," said Prince Secundus.

Prince Tertius waited for the other two to start on the way, and then he said, "Good-bye, Mom and Dad. I will do my best."

"Good-bye, son," said King Hilderic, who had a lump in his throat.

Queen Ermentrude hugged Prince Tertius, who then galloped after his two brothers.

It took the three princes a long time to reach the chief city of the empire. Their horses were very tired by then, and their clothes were quite worn out. They had also used up their money and had had to borrow from the treasurers of the kingdoms through which they passed.

"So far," said Prince Tertius sadly, "we've piled up a considerable debt, which makes our kingdom worse off than ever."

"After I've won the princess," said Prince Primus, "I will pay the debt three times over."

"I will pay it five times over," said Prince Secundus.

Prince Tertius said, "That's *if* one of us wins."

"How can we lose?" asked Princes Primus and Secundus together.

And indeed, when they arrived in the capital, they were greeted with kindness. They were given fresh horses and beautiful new clothing of the richest description, and were shown to a lavish suite in the largest and most beautiful palace they had ever imagined. Many servants were at their call, and all served them with the greatest politeness.

The three princes were very pleased with their treatment.

Prince Primus said, "The emperor must know what a wonderful family we come from. Our ancestors have been kings for many generations."

"Yes," said Prince Tertius, "but they have all been poor kings. I wonder if the emperor Maximian knows that."

"He must," said Prince Secundus. "Emperors know everything. Otherwise, how could they be emperors?"

The second assistant serving-maid was at that moment bringing in fresh towels so that the princes might take their baths in preparation for a great feast that night.

Prince Primus said at once, "You! Serving-maid!"

The serving-maid trembled at being addressed by a prince, and curtsied very low. "Yes, Your Highness."

"Is the emperor a wise emperor?"

The serving-maid said, "Oh, Your Highness, the entire empire marvels at his wisdom."

Prince Secundus said, "Would he care whether the princes who visit him are rich or poor?"

"Oh, no, Your Highness," said the serving-maid. "He is so wealthy that money means nothing to him. He is concerned only with the happiness of his daughter. If she asks to marry a certain prince, that prince will become heir to the kingdom even if he doesn't possess a single penny."

Prince Primus and Prince Secundus smiled and nodded to each other as though to say: We knew it all along.

Prince Tertius smiled at the serving-maid and said, "And what about the princess, my dear? Is she as pretty as you are?"

The serving-maid turned very pink and her mouth fell open. She seemed quite unable to speak.

Prince Primus said to his brother in a low voice, "Don't call her 'my dear.' It unsettles servants to be addressed so by a prince."

Prince Secundus said to his brother in an even lower

voice, "How can a serving-maid be pretty? A serving-maid is just a serving-maid."

Prince Tertius said, "Just the same, I would like an answer to my question."

The serving-maid, who was really quite pretty even though she was a serving-maid (but most princes wouldn't have noticed that), said, "Your Royal Highness must be joking. The princess is taller than I am and far more beautiful. She is as beautiful as the sun."

"Ah," said Prince Primus. "A rich princess who is as beautiful as the sun is someone to be interested in."

Prince Secundus said, "It would be quite a pleasure to have a rich princess like that about one's palace."

Prince Tertius said, "She might be too bright to look at, if she is as beautiful as the sun."

The serving-maid said, "But she is haughty."

Prince Primus said, at once, "A serving-maid may not speak unless she is spoken to."

Prince Secundus said, severely, "This comes of saying 'my dear' to serving-maids."

But Prince Tertius said, "Is she *very* haughty, my dear?"

"*Very* haughty, Your Highness," said the serving-maid, trembling at the haughty stares of the other two brothers. "There have been a number of princes who have already applied for her hand, but she would have none of them."

"Of course not," said Prince Primus. "They were probably pip-squeaks who couldn't bend an iron bar an inch. Why should she be interested in them?"

"Probably," said Prince Secundus, "they couldn't even lift a sword, let alone fight with one. She wouldn't be interested in them."

"Perhaps," said Prince Tertius, "we ought to ask the serving-maid what became of the princes who didn't please the princess."

The serving-maid's eyes dropped, and she said sadly, "They were all turned into statues, Your Highness. Handsome statues, for they were all young and handsome princes."

Prince Tertius shook his head. "I had hoped the emperor was only joking, but he must have really meant what he said on the parchment. Are there many of those statues?"

"There are about a dozen on each side of the garden path along which the princess walks each morning, Your Highness. She never looks at them, for she is as hard-hearted as she is beautiful."

"Pooh," said Prince Primus. "It doesn't matter that she is hard-hearted, as long as she is rich. And beautiful, too, of course. I shall soften her heart. . . . Now be off with you at once, serving-maid."

The serving-maid curtsied deeply and left the room, taking backward steps, for it would have been very impolite for her to turn her back on three princes.

* * *

That night there was a great feast, and the three princes were the guests of honor.

The emperor, seated on a splendid throne at the head of the table, greeted them. Next to him was the princess Meliversa, and she was indeed as beautiful as the sun. Her hair was long and the color of corn silk. Her eyes were blue and reminded everyone of the sky on a bright spring day. Her features were perfectly regular and her skin was flawless.

But her eyes were empty, and her face was expressionless.

She did not smile when Prince Primus was introduced to her. She looked at him proudly and said, "What kingdom are you from?"

He said, "I am from Micrometrica, Your Imperial Highness."

The princess said, with contempt, "I know all the kingdoms of Earth, and Micrometrica is the smallest of them." And she looked away from him.

Prince Primus backed away from her and took his seat at the table. He whispered to Prince Tertius, "She will grow interested once I show her what I can do."

Prince Secundus was introduced to her, and she said, "You are also from Micrometrica, I imagine."

"Yes, Your Imperial Highness. Prince Primus is my brother."

"Micrometrica is also the poorest kingdom on Earth. If you and your brother must share its wealth, you must be poor indeed." And she looked away from him.

Prince Secundus backed away from her and took his seat at the table. He whispered to Prince Tertius, "She will forget our poverty when I show her what I can do."

Prince Tertius was introduced to her, and she said, "Still another from Micrometrica?"

"We are triplets, Your Imperial Highness," said Prince Tertius, "though not identical ones. And what we have, we share."

"But you have nothing to share."

"We have no money and no power," said Prince Tertius, "but we and our kingdom are happy. And when happiness is shared, it increases."

"I have never noticed that," said the princess, and she looked away from him.

Prince Tertius backed away from her and took his seat at the table. He whispered to his brothers, "She is rich, and our country needs money. But her beauty is ice-cold and her wealth does not bring her happiness."

*   *   *

The next morning, Prince Primus made ready to put on a demonstration of his abilities for the princess. He had dressed in a fine pair of athletic shorts supplied by the emperor, and he made his magnificent muscles ripple as he stood before the mirror. He was quite satisfied with his appearance.

At that moment, however, there was a timid knock on the door, and when Prince Primus called, "Enter," the second assistant serving-maid came in with a bowl of apples.

"What is this?" demanded Prince Primus.

The serving-maid said, "I thought you might wish

some refreshment before undertaking your task, Your Highness."

"Nonsense," said Prince Primus. "I have all the refreshment I need. Take away those silly apples."

"I also wonder, Your Highness," said the serving-maid, blushing at her own daring in continuing to speak to him, "if you ought to undertake the task."

"Why not?" said Prince Primus, flexing his arms and smiling at himself in the mirror. "Do you think I am not manly enough?"

The serving-maid said, "You are certainly manly enough for anyone in the world but the princess. She is so hard to please, and it would be a shame that such a fine prince as Your Highness should be made into a marble statue."

Prince Primus laughed, scornfully. "She cannot be so hard to please that *I* do not please her—and that is enough talk. You must only speak when spoken to, serving-maid. Get out at once."

And the serving-maid got out at once, though she curtsied first.

*   *   *

Prince Primus stepped out into the large arena. Before him were the stands, covered by a beautiful silk canopy. The emperor was seated in the center, and at his right was the imperial princess Meliversa. The officials of the court were in the stands too, as were many a young gentleman and young lady. In one corner were Prince Secundus and Prince Tertius.

Prince Primus faced the stands, and around him was all the equipment he needed.

He turned, to begin with, to a large stack of barbells. The lighter ones he tossed aside lightly, even though an ordinary man might have had trouble lifting them.

Then he lifted the heavier ones, seizing them with both hands and bringing them up to his shoulders with a jerk, and then, more slowly, lifting them high in the air.

All the courtiers broke into applause when he managed to lift the heaviest weight that had been supplied. No other person had ever been known to lift that weight.

Finally, he bent an iron bar by placing it behind his neck and pulling the ends forward till they met in front of him. He then pulled the ends apart again, lifted the bar over his head, and threw it to one side.

Whatever he did brought round after round of applause from the courtiers. Even the emperor nodded approvingly. The princess, however, did not applaud; nor did she nod.

The emperor bent toward his daughter and said, "Really, my dear, this prince is quite the strongest man I have ever seen. It would be a pretty good thing to make him heir to the throne."

The princess said coldly, "It would be a pretty good thing to make him a strong man at the circus, My Imperial Father, but he is quite unsuitable for marriage to me. After all, do I have a set of weights in my chamber, or iron bars that need bending? I would quickly grow weary of watching him flex his arms, and if he tried to embrace me, he would break my ribs."

She rose in her seat, and at once everyone was quiet.

"Prince Primus," she said, in her beautiful voice.

Prince Primus folded his arms and listened confidently.

The princess said, "You are the strongest man I have ever seen, and I thank you for your efforts to please me. However, I do not wish you for my husband. You know the penalty."

She made a mystic pass with her hands (for she was a very well educated princess indeed), and there was a bright flash of light. The courtiers had covered their eyes, for they knew what to expect; but Prince Secundus and Prince Tertius were not prepared, and they were blinded for a moment by the flash.

When they recovered, they saw a statue being loaded into a cart so that it might be transported to the avenue in the garden along which the princess took her morning walk.

The statue was that of Prince Primus, arms folded, expression handsome and proud.

* * *

Prince Tertius was sad that evening. He had never lost a brother before, and he found he didn't like it.

He said to Prince Secundus, "I don't think Our Royal Father is going to like it either. And as for Our Royal Mother, she's going to hate it. How are we going to tell them?"

Prince Secundus said, "After I win the princess's hand, I may perhaps be able to persuade her to try to find a way to restore Our Royal Brother. After all, someone as well educated as she ought to be able to think of a way of doing so."

"But how will you be able to win her hand? She seems to have a heart of stone. Cold stone."

"Not at all," said Prince Secundus. "It's just that she wasn't interested in useless strength and muscles. What good is it to lift weights? Now *I* am a warrior. I can fight and handle weapons. That is a useful occupation."

"I hope so," said Prince Tertius, "but you will be taking a great chance. Still, the princess is rich, and we *do* need the money."

* * *

The next morning, Prince Secundus was arraying himself in gleaming armor when the second assistant serving-maid staggered in, carrying an enormous sword for him. She was bowed down by its weight, and when she tried to curtsy, she dropped it with a loud clang.

Prince Secundus said, with annoyance, "You are very clumsy."

"I beg your pardon, Your Highness," she said humbly, curtsying again, "but are you really going to undertake the task for the princess?"

"Certainly I am, but what business is that of yours, serving-maid?"

"None at all, Your Highness," admitted the serving-maid, "but the princess is so hard-hearted and so difficult to please. I do not want to see you turned into a statue, like your brother."

"I will not be turned into a statue," said Prince Secundus, "because the princess will be fascinated with
me. And now, serving-maid, leave my presence at once.
I cannot bear anyone as impertinent as you are."

The serving-maid curtsied and left.

* * *

Prince Secundus stepped out into the arena, and at
once there was applause from all the courtiers. The
armor that had been given him by the emperor was
beautiful and shiny, and fit him very well. His shield
was pure white, his sword was of the best steel, his
spear was perfectly balanced, and his helmet covered
his face and gave him a ferocious appearance.

He threw his spear, and it flew the length of the
arena and impaled itself in the center of a target.

Prince Secundus then challenged anyone at all to a
swordfight. A large man in armor came into the arena,
and for long minutes the two fought, sword clashing
on shield. But Prince Secundus could strike twice for
every once that his opponent could, and as the other
tired, Prince Secundus seemed to grow stronger. Soon
enough, the opponent raised his hands in surrender,
and Prince Secundus was the victor. The applause was
deafening.

Finally, Prince Secundus removed his helmet and
armor and mounted a horse. With one hand only, he
controlled the horse perfectly, making it rear on its
hind legs, leap, and dance. It was a remarkable per-
formance, and the audience went wild.

"Really, my dear," said the emperor, as he bent

toward his daughter, "this prince is an excellent warrior. He could lead my armies into battle and defeat all my enemies. Surely he must please you."

The princess's haughty face was cold, and she said, "He might make an excellent general if he also knew how to handle an army, but of what use would he be as a husband? There are no armed men in my chamber for him to fight, no horses for him to ride, no targets for him to shoot at. And if he forgot himself, he might throw his spear at me, since weapons are his greatest love and talent."

She rose in her seat, and at once everyone was quiet. She said, "Prince Secundus, you are the greatest warrior I have ever seen, and I thank you for your efforts to please me. However, I do not wish you for my husband. You know the penalty."

She made the same mystic pass as before. This time Prince Tertius knew enough to cover his eyes. When he took his hand away, there was another statue: that of a graceful, handsome prince with one hand raised as though it had just hurled a spear. Prince Tertius knew that he had lost a second brother.

* * *

Prince Tertius sat alone in the suite the next morning. He hadn't slept all night, and to tell the truth, he didn't know what to do.

He said to himself, "If I go home now, everyone will say I am a coward. Besides, how can I go home now and break the news to Dad? And dear Mom will weep for the rest of her life. As for me, I have lost two brothers who were good brothers to me, even if they were a little conceited and headstrong."

And now the second assistant serving-maid edged her way into the room. She had nothing in her hands.

Prince Tertius said, "Are you bringing me something, my dear?"

She curtsied very nervously and said, "No, Your Highness. Do not be angry with me, for I have only come to tell you that I asked both your brothers not to attempt the task, but they would not listen."

Prince Tertius sighed. "They were both very willful, I know. You mustn't blame yourself that they did not listen to you. And certainly I am not angry with you."

"Then, Your Highness, would *you* listen to me if I ask you not to attempt the task? You are not a great strongman or a great warrior. How can you win the cold, hard princess if your brothers could not?"

Prince Tertius said, "I know that all I can do is write a little poetry and sing a bit, but perhaps the princess might like that."

"She is very hard to please, Your Highness," said the serving-maid, shuddering at her impudence in arguing with a prince. "If you are made into a statue too, your parents will be left entirely without children, and they will have no heir to the throne."

Prince Tertius sighed again. "You are perfectly correct, little serving-maid. You have a kind heart and a thoughtful mind. But you see, our kingdom is so poor that Dad has to help in the garden and Mom has to help in the kitchen. If I could marry the princess, I would become so rich that I could make Mom and Dad and the whole kingdom happy. . . . So I think I *must* try to please the princess. Perhaps if I use my very best poems and sing them as sweetly as I can, she will be pleased."

Tears rolled down the serving-maid's cheeks. "Oh, how I wish she would, but she is so hard-hearted. If only she had *my* heart inside her, it would be different."

"Well then, my dear," said Prince Tertius, "let me test your heart. I will sing you some of my songs, and you can tell me if *you* like them. If you do, perhaps the princess will like them too."

The serving-maid was horrified, "Oh, Your Highness. You mustn't do that. Your songs are made to be sung to a princess, not to a simple serving-maid. How can you judge a princess by a serving-maid?"

"In that case," said Prince Tertius, "let us forget the princess, and I will ask only what the serving-maid thinks."

Prince Tertius tuned his lyre, one that was his own and that he had brought with him. Then, in a very soft and melodious voice, he sang a sad song of love denied. And when the serving-maid seemed to melt away in tears at the sadness, he sang a happy song of love attained, so that the tears vanished and she clapped her hands and laughed.

"Did you like them?" said Prince Tertius.

"Oh, yes," said the serving-maid. "The songs were

beautiful, and your voice made me feel as though I were in heaven."

Prince Tertius smiled. "Thank you, my lady." He bent and kissed her hand, and the serving-maid turned red with confusion and quickly put the hand he had kissed behind her back.

But just then there was a loud knock on the door, and there entered a chamberlain, a high court official, who bowed to Prince Tertius (but not very deeply) and said, "Your Highness, the imperial princess Meliversa wishes to know why you have not appeared in the arena."

He looked hard at the second assistant serving-maid as he said this, and the terrified young woman left the room hurriedly.

Prince Tertius said, "I do not know whether I will undertake the task. I am considering it."

The chamberlain bowed even less deeply than before and said, "I will inform the princess of what you have said. Please remain in this room until she decides what is to be done."

*   *   *

Prince Tertius waited in the room and wondered if the princess would turn him into a statue at once for hesitating over the task.

He was still wondering about it when the princess Meliversa entered the room. She did not knock. Imperial princesses never knock.

She said, "My chamberlain tells me that you might not undertake the task."

Prince Tertius said, "Your Imperial Highness may not like my poetry or my voice. It is all I have to offer."

"But if I do like them, what then?"

"In that case, I wonder if I wish to have as my wife someone who is so cold and hard-hearted, she is willing to turn brave, good princes into statues."

"Am I not beautiful, Prince?"

"It is an outside beauty, Imperial Princess."

"Am I not rich, Prince?"

"Only in money, Imperial Princess."

"Are you not poor, Prince?"

"Only in money, Imperial Princess, and I am used to it, actually, as are my parents and my kingdom."

"Do you not wish to be rich, Prince, by marrying me?"

"I think not, Imperial Princess. I am, after all, not for sale."

"And yet my chamberlain, on the other side of your door, heard you singing to a low-born serving-maid."

"That is true, but the serving-maid was tender-hearted and loving, and I wanted to sing to her. A tender and loving heart is, after all, the beauty and wealth I really want. If she will have me, then I will marry her, and someday, when I am king in my father's place, the low-born serving-maid will be my queen."

At that, the princess smiled. She was even more beautiful when she smiled. "Now," she said, "you will see the use of a good education."

She made a motion with her hand, muttered two or

three words, and with that she grew foggy in appearance, shrunk a little, changed a little—and Prince Tertius found himself looking at the second assistant serving-maid.

He said, in amazement, "Which are you, the imperial princess or the serving-maid?"

She said, "I am both, Prince Tertius. It was in the form of a serving-maid that I set myself the task of finding a suitable husband. Of what use was it to me what princes might do to win the hand of a beautiful and rich princess, not caring that she was cold and cruel. What I wanted was someone who would be kind and loving to a gentle, tenderhearted girl, even if she was not as beautiful as the sun or richer than gold. You have passed that test."

Again she changed and was the princess again, but a smiling, warm princess.

"Will you have me as wife now, Prince Tertius?"

And Prince Tertius said, "If you will remain always in your heart the gentle, loving woman I came to love, then I will marry you."

And with that all the princes who had been statues were suddenly brought back to warm flesh and blood again.

*   *   *

Prince Tertius and Princess Meliversa were married two months later, after the king and queen of Micrometrica were brought to the Imperial City by the very fastest coaches. They were as happy as anyone can imagine.

Prince Primus and Prince Secundus were also as happy as anyone can imagine, for they were alive again instead of being frozen in cold stone. They kept saying, "The serving-maid? We would never have imagined such a thing!"

Naturally, Prince Tertius was happy too, but the imperial princess was happiest of all. After all, she had been afraid that even with all her education she would never find anyone who would turn away from mere beauty and money, and love her for herself alone.

Little Green Men

by Barry B. Longyear

Jhanni caught his breath and rested in the shade of a boulder; he had found nothing. His father had forbidden him to search with the other Star Scouts for the UFO reported three days ago, and he wouldn't think of disobeying his father. Still, I said nothing about searching on my own, thought Jhanni.

"All this about 'invaders from outer space' is nonsense." His father had been unshakable on the subject, and nearly everybody thought the same way since the probe to Venus had reported no detectable life on the planet. Adventurer 7 had met with a mishap on its way to Saturn, and Jhanni's father had been furious. "More taxpayers' money thrown away on foolishness! We should spend the money to take care of problems here." Evidently the government felt the same way. When Jhanni turned thirteen the space program was canceled. Along with the program, the Star Scouts were officially scrapped.

Still, Jhanni's friends, and Star Scouts from all over, kept their squadrons alive to search for evidence—proof that would rekindle the space program and put them back on their road to the stars. Every time a UFO was reported, the squadron in that area would turn out and search for evidence—disturbed soil, burn marks, abandoned equipment—anything. But two years of searching had turned up nothing.

"Someday," Jhanni had told his squadron, "someday we'll find the proof we need, but until then we have to keep on trying." Nevertheless, one by one, the Star Scouts were leaving the squadron. Some, like Jhanni, were forbidden to waste good study time on such foolishness; others were discouraged; and still more had come to believe as their parents believed: Space travel costs too much to spend for uncertain returns. Jhanni's father had pulled him out of the squadron when his grades began to drop.

"We've had UFO reports for years. Spaceships, death rays and little green men from outer space, and it's always been something that could be explained. I don't want you ruining your education by wasting your time with it."

Jhanni loved his father, but he had argued with him for the first time in his life. "How do you know there's no life on other planets? Isn't it possible?"

"No one knows for sure, Jhanni, but I'll tell you this:

Before I believe it, someone's going to have to show me one of those little green men."

And that's what we're looking for, thought Jhanni, one of those little green men. He pushed away from the boulder and stepped into the sunlight. Shielding his eyes, he looked around. The squadron was searching the hills north of the development where the "object" was reported to have come down during the dust storm three days ago. His father wouldn't give his permission to join the search in the hills, and Jhanni was so angry it took him three tries to properly cycle the airlock on his home before stepping out into the desert.

He went south from the development to search the boulder field, although the "object" was reported north. The wind storm was blowing south that day, thought Jhanni. It's possible; not probable, but possible.

As he looked out over the boulder-strewn desert floor, the evening shadows grew long. Soon it would be dark and the desert cold. He checked the light buckle and heater in his belt and headed for his favorite boulder. At every turn he strained to glimpse the spaceship he hoped would be there. He knew he could get a better view from his boulder, the largest one in the field. It was pockmarked with great holes bored there by the action of the wind and sand, and Jhanni hadn't been there since he was a child playing with the friends who later became his mates in the Star Scouts.

Sometimes he would take one of his mother's blankets and some extra power cells and spend most of an icy night on his boulder, looking at the stars and dreaming of traveling among them. But the dreams became fewer as he grew older. There was no official interest anymore in moons, planets, stars or anything else that might cost the taxpayers more money.

As the sun dropped below the horizon, the stars appeared, and Jhanni watched them as he reached his boulder and climbed to the top. As he watched the countless pinpricks of light from unknown and unexplored stars, he let himself dream again of flying among them. His eyes glistened and he looked down. Maybe it is childish, he thought. The road to the stars is closed unless people can see the little green man in the flesh. And maybe . . . maybe the little green men don't exist after all.

Jhanni thought he heard a sound, and he looked over his shoulder. Seeing nothing unusual, he crawled over and around the boulder, looking into the tiny, windblown caves. There was nothing. He shrugged and stood atop the boulder, looking toward the development and his home. The outside light was on at his house, and his mother would scold him if he were late for dinner. He shook his head when he remembered he still had a tough stretch of homework to do and a math test in the morning. He knew he'd better pass this one. Too much imagination and not enough perspiration, his father would say if he failed. Taking one last look at the stars, Jhanni sighed and began to climb down from the boulder.

PING.

Jhanni froze. Slowly he turned his head in the direction of the sound. Deep in the shadow of a wind hole, a tiny light danced back and forth. Warily he crept toward the hole.

"HEY!"

Jhanni picked himself off the ground, knocked there by the suddenness of the sound. He reached to his belt and turned on his light buckle, aiming it at the hole. Inside there was a small, white cylinder propped up on spindly legs supported by round pads. The cylinder was dented, and its legs looked bent and battered.

"Turn off the light! I can't see."

Jhanni turned off his light buckle, and as his widening eyes adjusted again to the dark, tiny lights on the cylinder appeared and illuminated the hole. On one side of the object a tiny door opened, and a small, white-clad creature emerged, looked around and climbed down a tiny built-in ladder to the bottom of the wind hole. Jhanni peered closely as the creature lifted something and aimed it in Jhanni's direction.

"Can you hear me?"

"Uh . . ."

"Hold it." The creature adjusted a knob on its chest. "Had to lower the volume a bit. Good thing you dropped by; I only have a day's life support left."

"Uh . . ." Jhanni tried to untie his tongue, a million

questions in his mind competing for the first answer. "Are you . . . are you from up there?" He pointed up. "How can you talk to me, and where . . . ?"

"One thing at a time. That's where I come from, and I'm talking to you through a universal translator. I rigged it up with a speaker from the lander console in case anyone came by."

"What happened?"

The creature threw up its tiny arms. "What didn't? I've been out of touch with my base ever since the wind blew me into this hole three days ago, damaging my oxygen regulator and radio. I'm running a little short. Can you get me to an oxygen-enriched atmosphere?"

"Well . . . there's my gas box. I raise tropical insects, and they're oxygen absorbing. I did it for a school project in biochem once, and . . ."

"Do the bugs eat meat?"

"Oh. Well, I can put them in another container. Can you fly or anything? My home's quite a walk from here."

"I guess you better carry me, but take it easy."

"I will." Jhanni picked up the little creature and held it in his hand, surprised at its weight. It was only as tall as one of Jhanni's fingers. He could just barely see the creature shaking his head inside his tiny helmet.

"I can't get over how big you Martians are. Wait until Houston hears about this!"

Jhanni laughed. "If you think I'm big, wait until you see my father!" And wait until my father gets a load of you, thought Jhanni. "By the way, creature, what color are you under that suit?"

"My name's Frank Gambino, Captain, United States Air Force. I'm sort of brown; why?"

"No special reason." Jhanni slipped the tiny creature into his pocket and began climbing down from the boulder. The little man isn't green, thought Jhanni, but he'll do. As he reached the desert floor and started to run home, he stopped himself just in time from patting his pocket.

Selena's Song

by Elyse Guttenberg

Selena sat beside the large, wood-framed bed, holding tight to her mother's hand. Two weeks ago her mother had been well, out in the garden, weeding and singing her songs. Selena had been inside the house and so had not seen the dragon's shadow darkening the valley. But her mother had. And from the moment Esthella raised her head from the flower bed and heard the dragon's vengeful cry, nothing had gone well.

In the beginning, her mother had only felt tired, coming in from the garden earlier than usual to rest. But from there the drowsiness had turned to sleep, the sleep to fever. Now her mother's brown hair clung to her damp forehead, and Esthella, who once sang the nightingale's morning song as a gift to a queen, no longer had the strength to raise her voice.

The dragon had come for Prince Oriah, the news from the castle proclaimed. Five long days the prince had traveled on his proving quest, northward, toward the mountains. And when on the last day, Oriah scaled the peaks and found the dragon gone from its lair, he settled on the simpler task and destroyed its clutch of six golden eggs.

But no one, neither prince nor wizard, can outrun a dragon, and Oriah had scarcely reached the city gates when the dragon's magic song was heard overhead. Within the hour, the king's word was law. The prince's life must not be risked against the dragon. Instead, every man and woman able to bear weapons must join forces behind the king and his knights.

Selena's father had waited until the last possible moment. Now, Joran circled the house, calculating in his troubled heart the number of days he might be gone. And though his bearded jaw was firmly set, and the laughter that usually followed him was silent, he tried hard not to speak of his worries.

"That should do it now, daughter," he said. "The king's troops will be marching within the hour, and I must be counted in their numbers. I trust you, you know. And I leave it to you to take care of your mother. Have her drink the broth when she wakes. And sing for her, a little."

Selena stared down at her hands. "I could never sing as well as mother," she whispered. "Besides, I want to go with you and fight the dragon."

"Hush, daughter. You're too young to speak of fighting." Joran took Selena's hands in his. "And your voice is more than fair, but it's young. Like your arm, it will flourish in its own time. Waiting is always the hardest part, I know. And no one likes to be left behind. But if King Leonard will not let Prince Oriah risk his life, neither will I let you risk yours. It would be no lie if I told you I wished he'd never begun this business of questing after dragons."

"And I wish he'd never found the eggs!"

"Yes, but you can't tell that to him. It's in a prince's nature to think he must prove himself to the world."

"But didn't he know the mother dragon would follow?"

"Who's to say what's in a dragon's mind, Selena? Now stop worrying. One more battle and the dragon will be dead. I promise." Joran leaned down and hugged Selena; then, noticing a tangle in his wife's necklace, he bent to straighten it. It was the minstrel medallion Esthella always wore. On its face a young man juggled the earth's music. "Sing to her," Joran said again. "It's the one thing that keeps her safe." And with that, he stepped out into the strange twilight.

Each day since then, Selena had sat beside her mother, singing whatever verses came to mind. And though she could not hear it herself, with each song her voice blossomed and grew stronger, and each note was as sharp as the dagger she hoped would soon pierce the dragon's heart.

Sometimes, near the height of noon, when the sun was strong enough to crack the dragon's magic shadow, Esthella found the strength to join in. Selena would follow, working to match her mother's voice, melody and harmony blending into a beautiful whole. They sang songs they had not thought of since Selena had been a child, garden songs, and earth songs, ballads of distant kings and queens. They took turns dividing the verses into rounds, ballads, and lullabies. And they took comfort from the songs, knowing that the great seas had been crossed before, and dragons slain.

But always, when her mother slept, Selena tiptoed over to the mantel and dragged down her father's sword, the one that had accompanied him on his own proving quest. The sword was narrow and sharp, nearly as tall as she, with a simple hilt of inlaid silver. Each day she measured its weight against the strength of her fist. Steadying herself, she'd wrap both hands around the hilt, and with a heaving breath, raise the heavy sword from the floor. At first the work proved too much, but Selena would not be discouraged. She had made her decision. If Prince Oriah would not fight this dragon, she would.

One afternoon, Selena's mother woke from a feverish dream. "Selena," she called weakly. "It's so dark. Is it night already?"

Selena shook her head. Day after day the murky shadow had been spreading across the sky. And her mother had not been the only one to fall under its gloom. Where they could, other families had boarded up their homes and run away to relatives in distant villages. Only yesterday, Selena had watched Maury, the widow who sold them herbs, drive her small wagon down the road, the goats and cow straggling behind, while the youngest son walked with a lantern in his hand.

Sadly, Selena said, "It's the dragon's magic, Mother, same as it touched you. There's no daylight in the sky. The soldiers must be waiting it out, don't you think, because they can't fight in the dark? But Father said not to worry. He said they would fight the dragon. He promised."

"Is it so much worse, then?" Esthella lay back on her pillows.

"I'm sorry, Mother. I shouldn't have frightened you." Selena glanced up at her father's sword. Soon, she decided, she must tell her mother of her plans to fight the dragon.

But then, because Selena could not bear to see the pain in her mother's eyes, she sang. And sometimes Esthella would raise her hand, pointing out a note that ought to be lengthened, a word sung slightly higher. They passed the hour that way, one voice weak, the other clear and lovely, until the darkness was forgotten and her mother's heavy eyes closed into sleep again.

Selena watched carefully; then, certain that her mother would not soon waken, she pulled the sword down from the mantelpiece. She had been working hard with it each day, pushing herself. She could raise it up high above her head now, swing it in a broad circle and lower it down again, without her arm cramping from effort. But that was all. Try as she might, she still was not strong enough to thrust and parry, to swing and backblade.

As she stood there planning, there was a loud knocking at the door. Quickly, she laid the sword aside. The knock came again, and this time Selena's mother forced herself up out of sleep and nodded for Selena to open the door.

A tall, dark-haired soldier stood outside, his wide shoulders filling the doorway. "King's orders, miss," he said, his voice coarse but well-intentioned. "Everyone who's still in the village is to move up the hill to the castle. It's for your own protection."

"Move? But we can't move. My mother's ill. She can't walk."

The man peered over Selena's head until he found Esthella. "Sorry, ma'am," he continued. "I'm instructed to say that the gates will be open from noon till eve, today and tomorrow. After that, you're on your own."

Esthella rose up on one elbow. "Tell me, sir. Is there any other news? Has the king seen the battle?"

"Oh, he tried, ma'am. Don't believe anyone tells you different. But the archers couldn't shoot their bows. The wood went limp. It's like the earth is cursed. And I'll tell you the truth of it, we don't like it. None of us."

"But the soldiers? The king has sent his soldiers?"

"Into the meadows, ma'am. And they haven't returned, not a one of them. Though the king swears they're not dead. For no one ever heard a sound of battle or a single cry."

Mother and daughter looked at each other. "And has the king sent his wizard?" Esthella asked.

"Oh, certainly. But his magic's spoilt, ma'am. I was with him myself, his bowman on the right. He was dressed in all his wizard's finery, cape billowing, staff raised. Arel, that's his name, he spoke three words. Words of power. I wouldn't know how to repeat them even if I wanted to, ma'am, and that I don't. But a cloud of fire went up. Real fire. I felt it myself. Arel pointed his finger toward the dragon, and the cloud followed after."

"What happened?" Esthella's voice grew sharp with waiting.

The soldier shook his head. "Nothing, ma'am. Except that the dragon sent out a growl, though it was more like a song, if you ask me. With its own kind of sad beauty. But deafening. And the wizard's fire withered. Turned to smoke. After that, wasn't anything even the wizard could do."

"A song, did you say?" Selena asked, wondering.

"Yes, miss. And I hope to the sweet earth I never hear it again."

When the soldier was gone and her mother napping once again, Selena ran for the chest that stood at the foot of her mother's bed. Quickly she began searching, tossing everything aside until, at last, buried near the bottom, she found a bolt of waxed linen. Starting at one end, Selena tore off two narrow strips, rolled them tightly, and stuffed them into her pocket, nodding to herself. She would take a candle, and leather gauntlets since she had no real armor. The waxed linen for earplugs because, just possibly, no one had thought to try that. And the sword, of course, for whatever it proved to be worth. But when Selena moved to sling her father's sword over her shoulder, it bumped against a corner of the table, and her mother sat up.

For one long moment there was silence. Then, "Where are you going?" Esthella asked.

Selena held her back straight. "It's no use trying to get you to the castle, Mother. And I won't leave you behind to save myself. I'm going to find the dragon."

"My love!" Esthella shook her head. "You weren't raised to be a warrior. How can you succeed where the prince failed?"

"The prince never tried! No one has. I know I've no royal blood, and I don't have a warhorse, or a wizard's power to protect me. But there must be something I can do."

"You've thought about this?"

Selena nodded.

"And you're not afraid?"

"Well, not exactly. I mean, of course I'm afraid. But I have to try."

Esthella looked for a long time at her daughter. "Well," she said, managing a smile. "I suppose I'd have been disappointed if any daughter of mine thought differently. But please, wear my necklace. It's a minstrel's necklace. It's filled with memories, not magic. But more than once, it gave me courage. Perhaps it will do the same for you."

Proudly Selena slipped the long chain over her head. "Mother," she asked. "Do you think a dragon could sing? The soldier said it almost sounded that way."

Esthella's voice grew hazy. "Possibly. A dragon mourning its lost eggs might."

Within the hour, Selena had slipped into the darkness outside. She glanced once toward the castle, wondering which window Prince Oriah hid behind. Then, choosing the wide, main road for herself, Selena started for the hill where the dragon camped.

The closer she came to the dragon, the thicker the darkness grew, until, as she passed the outer city gates and approached the open meadow, she could hardly see at all. The next moment, she tripped over a rock. That's odd, she thought. This meadow was cleared. Selena brushed herself off, walking slower now, one hand stretched out in front of her as if she were blind. But she tripped again, her head banging hard against the sword on her back. This time Selena reached inside her quilted jacket for the slim candle she had brought, lit it, then surveyed the meadow.

Ahead of her, the path was strewn with fallen bodies. They lay with their faces to the earth, some curling snail-like, others with their arms all askew. Selena lowered herself to one knee and searched the first man's face. "Let it not be you, Father," she whispered. But the man she saw was a stranger, neither dirty, nor wounded in battle, nor dead. The man moaned as she prodded his shoulder, but he did not look up. He was asleep, felled, as the king's messenger had said, by the dragon's cry. There had never been a chance for battle. Selena ran up to the next man, and the next and the next. They were all asleep, crumpled and snoring, their hunched backs littering the meadow.

Selena wanted nothing more than to search for her father, but she dared not. From this vantage, the darkness appeared to be tightening over the city. The air had a thick musty smell that burned against the back of her throat. Shielding the candle's glow with her hand, Selena hurried on.

At last, stretched out across the rise of the opposite hill, she found the dragon's dim silhouette. Its long back hugged the hilltop. Its head and tail snaked down toward each other, so long they almost met under the great, smooth swell of stomach. The dragon's blue wings were folded down now, delicate as a spider's web, and from its nostrils two thin lines of steam rose like arrows shooting toward the sky.

Selena stepped back. For all her bravery, she had never imagined the beast would be so huge, the malice in its eyes so cold and hungry. If she had doubted before, she knew now; she could never kill the dragon alone. Though perhaps, with luck, she still might trick it. If only the sword would do its part and her throat not burn too harshly.

She tightened the belt of her jacket and carefully set her mother's necklace on top, where she could see it. Then quickly, before she lost courage, Selena drew her sword and plunged it point first into the earth.

"Dragon!" Selena cried, hands on her sword so the dragon would think she meant to fight. "Arise and fight, weapon to weapon."

Through half-open lids, the dragon gazed down at Selena. With a sound that could only be laughter, it shot two fiery breaths toward the meadow. The wind burned like a midnight bonfire against her face, but it was a warning only, and Selena stood her ground. "Bring Prince Oriah to me," the dragon bellowed. "When I have picked the last of his bones clean, then we will talk of swordfights, not before."

"No!" Selena shouted back. "As long as you fight with magic, Prince Oriah will not come."

The dragon cocked its sleek head to one side, as if to measure the length of Selena's sword and decide whether this small girl posed any threat. At last, the dragon spoke again, its voice low and gravelly. "Who will come then, lady? You? When your king has traded his son for the eggs he destroyed, then I will fight you."

Selena felt the weight of the necklace hanging against her chest. All of the earth's music, she reminded herself, was balanced in the minstrel's hands. Her mother had wanted her to remember that, else why would she have given her the necklace? But did that mean dragons loved music? And if so, what kind of music?

Somehow she had to make the dragon come closer.

If it used its magic now, she would be as helpless as her mother. Selena cupped her hands to her mouth. "Are you afraid of one girl and one sword?" she cried, lunging forward, with a challenge she hoped the dragon could not ignore.

"Afraid?" the dragon bellowed, its pride offended. "I am afraid of nothing." And the giant shook itself free of the hilltop and sprang into the air, exactly as Selena had hoped. Overhead, she saw the dragon's belly, pale against the blackened sky. Its scales were larger than her hands and so dense, she feared no mortal sword could ever bring it down.

Higher and higher the dragon climbed. Then, as its flight widened into an arc and Selena felt certain it was not watching, she snatched the two linen strips from her pocket and pushed one firmly into each ear. There was no longer any wind, no sound of the dragon's heavy breathing. The world had grown quiet.

"Come closer," she whispered. "Closer."

As if to answer, the dragon began its dive, spiraling lower and lower, its taloned wings angled to catch the wind. With her eyes, Selena saw the dragon open its great mouth. With her eyes, she saw its forked tongue rising and falling as the dragon spoke the magic words that had sent the soldiers to sleep. But with her ears, she heard nothing. The dragon's spell could not reach her.

Curious, the dragon slowed its flight, until finally it hovered just above Selena's head. No mere human had ever withstood its spell before, certainly not at so close a range. "Draw your sword, girl, as you stand there, or I shall sing thy death song now," it hissed.

Though she could not hear its voice, Selena guessed well what the dragon said. But instead of answering its challenge, she began to sing, gently, picking her words with care, for she was not certain what kind of music would sooth a dragon's troubled heart:

> *"Not wind nor rain nor mournful cry*
> *Can steal the sunlight from the sky,*
> *But only hide what children know,*
> *Awaits above the midnight foe."*

The dragon's green eyes narrowed. Selena's voice sounded as familiar as a gentle wind in the treetops, surely not something a dragon need fear. "Why do you wait, foolish child?" it asked. "Take up your sword. Do you want to die without soldier's honor?"

But Selena only stood as she was, hands patient on the sword. As long as she could not hear the dragon, its magic could not affect her. And if she guessed correctly, the dragon would not kill her until she had actually drawn the sword to fight. Again, she began to weave the notes of a song, louder now, as she lured the dragon down.

> *"The night is warm, thy bed is soft*
> *No one shall harm thy sleeping loft.*
> *To tame the heart of dragon friend,*
> *I raise my song to battle's end.*

Will you who dare a magic spell
Agree to stop thy song as well?"

The notes were soft, the words so simple. Surely, the dragon thought, there could be no harm in listening a little longer. The dragon let out a long breath of air, a sigh almost. And this time, no angry fire surged from its throat.

Selena watched closely. She almost dared hope the dragon's tail moved more sluggishly. Its wings no longer seemed to beat the air so harshly. Cautiously, she removed the cloth from her ears.

"Was that a song?" the dragon asked, its voice wistful and slow. For two long weeks it had lain awake, keeping its magic strong. But sleep seemed such a pleasant thing now, with the music so close. Perhaps it could sleep for just a little while without its spells breaking, just a short nap before its next two-week sleep began in earnest. . . .

In her softest voice, Selena said, "It's only a song my mother sang at night."

The dragon, lulled into memory, dropped gracefully to the ground. "I too sang for my clutch of eggs, before Prince Oriah destroyed them," it said, nestling its chin into a grassy spot beside Selena's feet.

"Will you not let me sing my mother's song?" Selena asked carefully. "Once more, before I die?" If the dragon suspected anything now, she thought, there would be no chance of escape. It was too close. Too huge.

"I never knew humans could sing so sweetly," the

dragon yawned. Later there would be time to fight this girl. After she had sung her songs. For now, it wouldn't matter if it stretched itself out to listen. Just to one song.

The dragon's tail patted the ground. Selena closed her fist around the necklace and took a breath. Her voice came steady and true, filled with the strength of new springtimes, or rivers rushing over their courses. She made a lullaby of the garden outside her window, of her father's laughter and of the simple things she knew. She sang with the voice her mother had promised she would someday have, rich and mellow as a nightingale's morning song.

And as she sang, the dragon listened, its gaze turning more and more inward, its heavy eyelids blinking. Once. Twice. And then no more.

The dragon was asleep.

Selena sang for a while longer. Then slowly, softly, she let her melody trail away, part of the wind again.

The dragon did not rise.

"Now," she said, noticing for the first time the thin streak of light opening across the eastern sky. "I have done my part. Oriah can finish his."

The sword Selena left where it was. Later she would come back for it. It was too heavy to carry around anyway, she decided.

Humming softly, Selena started down the hill to find her father.

The King's Dragon

by Jane Yolen

There was once a soldier who had fought long and hard for his king. He had been wounded in the war and sent home for a rest.

Hup and one. Hup and two. He marched down the long, dusty road, using a crutch.

He was a member of the Royal Dragoons. His red and gold uniform was dirty and torn. And in the air of the winter's day, his breath plumed out before him like a cloud.

Hup and one. Hup and two. Wounded or not, he marched with a proud step. For the Royal Dragoons are the finest soldiers in the land and—they always obey orders.

After a bit, the soldier came upon a small village. House after house nestled together in a line.

"Just the place to stop for the night," thought the dragoon to himself. So he hupped and one, hupped and two, up to the door of the very first house. He blew the dust from his uniform, polished the medals on his chest with his sleeve till they clinked and clanked together and shone like small suns. Then he knocked on the door with his crutch.

Now that very first house belonged to a widow and she, poor woman, was slightly deaf. When she finally heard the sound of the knock, she called out in a timid voice: "Who is there?"

The soldier puffed out his chest. He struck his crutch smartly on the ground. "I am a Royal Dragoon," he said, "and I am tired and hungry and would like to come in."

The woman began to shake. "The royal *dragon?*" she cried, for she had not heard him clearly. "I did not know the king had one. But if it *is* a dragon, and hungry besides, I certainly do not want him here. For he will eat up all I have and me as well!" She so frightened herself that she threw her apron up over her head and called out, *"Go away!"* Then weeping and wailing, she ran out her back door to her neighbor's home.

The Royal Dragoon did not see her leave, of course. But as she had told him to go, go he did, for the Royal Dragoons are the finest soldiers in the land and—they always obey orders.

Hup and one. Hup and two. He marched to the second house and knocked on the door. He stood at attention, his chest puffed out, and in the cold, wintry air, his breath plumed out before him like a cloud.

Now that second house belonged to the widow's

father, and he, poor man, was nearly blind. He listened to his daughter's story, and when the knock came, the two of them crept up to the window. She still had her apron up over her head, and he could see no farther than the end of his nose. They peered out, and all they saw was the great plume of breath coming from the soldier's mouth.

"See," said the daughter, "it *is* a dragon. And he is breathing smoke."

"Who is there?" called out the old man in a timid voice.

"I am a Royal Dragoon," said the soldier. As he spoke, even more clouds streamed from his mouth. "I am tired and hungry and would like to come in."

"*Go away!*" cried the old man. "No one is here." Then he and his daughter ran out the back way to their neighbor's house, weeping as they went.

The Royal Dragoon did not see them leave, of course. But as he had been told to go, go he did, for the Royal Dragoons are the finest soldiers in the land and—they always obey orders.

Hup and one. Hup and two. He marched to the third house and knocked on the door. He stood at attention, his chest puffed out, and saluted so smartly, his medals clinked and clanked together.

Now the third house belonged to the mayor, and a very smart young mayor he was. He could see perfectly well. He could hear perfectly well. And when the widow and her father finished their story, the mayor said: "The king's dragon, eh? And just listen to that!

I hear his scales clinking and clanking together. He must be terribly hungry indeed and ready to pounce."

So the mayor called out the door, "*Wait*, Sir Dragon." Then the mayor and the widow and the widow's father ran out the back. They gathered together all the other people in the town, and without even taking time to pick up their belongings, they ran and ran as fast as they could, until they came to the mountains, where a very real dragon lived. When it came out and ate them all up, not a one of them was surprised. They were already convinced of dragons, you see.

As for the Royal Dragoon, he stood waiting at attention in front of the third house for a very, very, very long time. He may be standing there still. For the Royal Dragoons are the finest soldiers in the land. And—they always obey orders.

Voices in the Wind

by Elizabeth S. Helfman

At the window of his cottage by the sea sat old Tom Anthony. His eyes were in a dream, and he held his head a little to one side, listening, it seemed, to something far away but very pleasant to his hearing. His wife, Sarah, set down a bowl of sauerkraut on the table in the center of the room. She felt suddenly very lonely. There sat Tom, as he had every afternoon and evening, ever since he had been too old to go out fishing. It was worse for her than when he used to be away all day. Then she had expected no companionship. Only occasionally he would come home with a lost look in his eyes and a fantastic tale of the wind and the sea on his lips. She would forgive him, and laugh. And he laughed with her.

He was so different now, content to merely sit and listen to nothing. It was strange, too, that he no longer sought out old Jonah, who lived across the fence at the south. So often, before, they would tell and re-tell long tales of the sea and hazardous fishing.

"Tom, your supper is ready."

She had called him just like this for so many days. He came, as she had known he would, slowly, with a look of childlike apology. "I ought to be more talkative, I suppose, Sarah. I'm sorry."

They sat at the table in silence, and the food stood waiting. Time hesitated for a moment, then went on again. Sarah was a little afraid.

"Tom, why do you sit at the window every day, so long, staring out and looking lost, as if you were listening to something? You seem so far away, you might as well be miles out at sea."

Tom looked at her apologetically. "I'm sorry, Sarah, and I'd tell you but you'd think me crazy."

"I'll think you worse than crazy if you go on this way, Tom. Tell me!"

Tom leaned his elbows on the table so suddenly that the candle flame trembled. The shadows in the corner of the room drew back. "All right, Sarah, I'll tell you."

Sarah bent forward eagerly. "Yes, Tom."

"It's the wind, Sarah, and the sea."

"Tom, haven't you heard enough of the wind and the sea all your life without spending hour after hour listening to them now?"

"It's different now, Sarah. I never knew until some weeks ago that the wind has words to say when it runs about outside the house and cries and moans around the corners. If you listen long enough you can hear what the sea, too, is saying as it comes tumbling in, one wave after another."

Sarah's face was blank. But Tom kept on.

"It tells secrets to the old pines, Sarah."

"You *are* crazy, Tom Anthony."

"Why shouldn't the wind say something, Sarah, when it goes crying about, always restless, as if it were searching for something?"

He *is* crazy, thought Sarah. The thought went through her head over and over again, dully, like a headache.

"I said you'd call me crazy, Sarah."

What should she do with him now? she wondered.

"Come with me to the window and listen," he begged.

"Tom, it's witches, or—or something. Oh, Tom! *Are* you crazy?"

He was silent; then he sighed a little and finished eating. The same thought went through Sarah's head over and over again—what should she do?

* * *

Of course Sarah did nothing about it. Somehow thinking that Tom was a little crazy did not make things much different from what they were before. Only now he pleaded with her every evening to come with him to the window and listen. He wanted so much for her to believe.

At last one evening she went to the window with him and sat there a long time, her hand in his, listening.

"Do you hear them, Sarah?"

"Yes, I hear them, not being deaf But no words, Tom, no words."

He was disappointed, but he was not less confident. "Listen again," he said.

She listened. "No words, Tom."

Nevertheless, after that she went to the window with him every evening, to sit there quietly and listen, even if there were no words to hear. She felt closer to Tom that way, and she was sure he felt closer to her. On evenings when there was no wind she could feel the loneliness in them both.

Sarah had almost forgotten that she thought Tom crazy. And yet, when she took time to think about it, she supposed he must be a little simple minded. For she could not hear words in the wind's moaning, nor a message in the sea's murmurs.

"Can't you hear them, Sarah? Can't you?" Tom would ask.

On an evening in July there was a wild wind wandering about the house, and the sea roared loud on the shore. Tom left his supper before he was half finished to go to the window and listen. Sarah washed the dishes, dried them, and followed. They sat there a long time, Tom with an expression of ecstasy on his face, Sarah passive and rather tired. The wind and the sea roared, echoed each other, roared again. Suddenly an expression of wonder and a kind of terror came to Sarah's face.

"Tom!"

She seized his arm.

"Tom, I thought I heard—"

Tom was not disturbed, not surprised. A triumphant smile spread over his face.

"Of course you heard them, Sarah."

She was silent again, listening. What was it the wind said? She couldn't be sure. Oh, it was all nonsense. And yet . . .

"Tom, am I crazy, too?"

He laughed. "It doesn't matter—if we *both* are— does it?"

She could hear only a word now and then, but there was no denying it. After a while she grew weary of sitting there and went to bed, a little afraid but very happy. Tom followed much later, softly whistling a strange tune she had never heard before.

* * *

Sarah had to listen many times, hour after hour, while the wind went around the house, before she was sure of the words it used. She was almost as eager to listen as Tom, though she always washed the dishes and put them away before she went to the window.

One night, when they were listening together, the words of the wind came clearer than ever before. They made a chant like this;

> *"The wind is wild with wandering,*
> *Wild with moaning through the trees,*
> *Wild with whispering in the pines,*
> *Wild with crying to the sea. . . .*

The wind is wild with wandering,
Over the troubled sea again,
Whistling around the house again.
I am the wind,
The wandering wind."

Sarah smiled somewhat foolishly and murmured,
" 'The wind is wild with wandering.' Who could have
known . . . ?"

Tom was listening to still other words, for a gentle
rain was falling. And he heard the rain say:

"I come with murmurs,
Murmurs,
Out of the clouds that know the thunder,
Out of the sea that roars and tumbles,
Down to the earth that waits and wonders—
I am the murmuring rain."

"The rain sings, too, Sarah," Tom said.

The rain kept on murmuring. The wind in its wandering blew open the door, put out the candle, and left
Tom and Sarah in sudden darkness. He took her hand
in his and they stood there in that darkness, silent and
unafraid.

*   *   *

There was a day in late July when an unexpected
rain came out of a sky that had been still and blue an
hour before. Tom and Sarah were at the window, listening to what the angry rain might say, when there

was a knock at the door. Sarah was afraid, why she did not know.

"I won't go, Tom. I won't."

He crossed to the door and opened it. On the doorstep stood a teenage boy, wet all over, with little rivulets running from the ends of his long, blond hair.

Tom recognized him—Oliver Trowbridge, from the nearby summer resort. He had taken Oliver sailing many times and let him dangle a line over the edge of the boat until he caught a fish or two.

Oliver ambled in, past Tom, to the fireplace, where Tom had built a roaring fire against the dampness. "Whew!" he said. "I thought you'd never get to the door. I got soaked in all this rain, and I thought you'd let me dry off for a minute or two."

Suddenly Sarah hated Oliver Trowbridge. He had come just when she had been listening to catch a few words the rain said. Now he stood there by the fire as if it were his own, babbling things she had no patience with. But she said only, "You're welcome here. Would you like something to eat?" And she brought out a dish of her sauerkraut.

"Oh," said Oliver. "Thanks." After a slow start he ate it eagerly.

Sarah saw that Tom was at the window looking out, no longer listening to Oliver. And yet she knew he was not content to have him there.

"What's the matter with the old man?" Oliver gulped his last mouthful. "Is he deaf?"

"No, he's not deaf. He's listening to things you'd be glad to hear, if you could."

"Oh, of course. Yes, of course," Oliver drawled. Then he smiled and crossed to the window, where he stood beside Tom. He put one hand on Tom's shoulder and received no answer. He touched Tom's shoulder, again with no success. Feeling playful, he pulled Tom's ear, very gently.

Tom turned to him angrily. "What do you want with me?"

Oliver answered, "I want to know what it is you're listening to."

"You won't believe, but if you want to know—I listen to what the wind says, what the sea mumbles, what the rain murmurs when it comes out of the clouds."

Oliver laughed long and loud. "Well, let me listen with you, old man."

Tom turned back to the window. Oliver stood beside him, minute after minute. Then he said, "All I hear is a little bit of rain falling, a little bit of ocean coming in, the way it always does, and the wind blowing around. No words."

"I wouldn't expect *you* to hear them."

"Does your wife hear them?"

Sarah nodded emphatically. "Of course."

Oliver broke again into shrill laughter, then stopped as suddenly as he had begun. "Well, I'll be going. The rain's about over. But first, let me tell you this—if you really think you hear any words in the sound of wind, and rain, and sea, you are absolutely crazy. Absolutely."

Tom turned to the window again, as if he wished he had not heard. Sarah smiled to herself, as if she knew things Oliver could never dream of. And he mistook her smile.

"Oh, I suppose you've been fooling all this time," he said. "You *were* clever. For a while I thought you really meant it. Time to go. Good-bye, everybody!" And he was gone.

"What a fool!" said Sarah. Tom nodded in agreement. "Of course *he* couldn't hear the voices, not even wanting to believe."

"Of course not."

They went to listen again and heard the wind murmuring, *I am the wind, the wind that murmurs in the pines.*

*   *   *

They were troubled, though. Tom felt for the first time that it would be pleasant to hear someone besides Sarah and himself swear to the truth of the words in the wind's voice. And so he sought out old Jonah the next day. He found him sitting in a corner of his kitchen, looking out to the sea and dreaming.

Jonah woke from dreaming to astonishment when he saw Tom. "Well, Tom! Where have you been all this time? I thought likely you'd fallen into the sea and drowned, or something even better!" He laughed heartily, as if this were the greatest joke in the world.

Tom shook his head. "No, I've simply been at home, listening to things."

"Well, Tom," said Jonah cheerfully, "I guess that's about all there is to do now that we can't go fishing anymore."

Tom was thoughtful. "I suppose no one around here knows more about the sea than you do, Jonah."

Jonah laughed again, finding this an even greater joke. "You're right, Tom, I reckon no one could know more about the sea than old Jonah."

"Well, have you ever heard the wind at sea telling you things?"

"Of course, and you have, too, Tom. It used to tell me when I'd better make for home instead of being caught in a storm and when it would be safe to steer north."

"But, Jonah, did the wind ever *speak* to you? Did you ever hear words in its voice?"

"Of course not, and neither did you, Tom."

"Not until a few weeks ago. But now both Sarah and I listen at the window when the wind is blowing, and it chants strange words."

Old Jonah laughed comfortably. "What a queer thing to dream about."

"It's not a dream, Jonah. We've listened hour after hour and we hear what the wind says, the sea, and the rain."

"Sarah hears this, too?"

"Both of us."

"No one knows more about the sea and the wind

than I do, and I never heard any words. You're getting old, Tom, getting old. And so is Sarah. Perhaps you've both become a little simple. That makes me sad. You used to be one of the best fishermen on the coast."

* * *

That night there was again a wind, and Tom and Sarah went to listen to its song. But they remembered Oliver with his scornful laughter, and the careless disbelief of old Jonah. Tom heard some of the words the wind said, but Sarah's thoughts were so busy that she heard none of them.

The night after that there was also a wind. Tom and Sarah were troubled as they sat at supper.

"He was a fool, that Oliver person," grumbled Tom. "And old Jonah, he's a good enough old man, but he can't have listened to the wind for very long."

Sarah nodded. "Oliver was crazy. And old Jonah pretty near it, I guess."

"And yet," said Tom, suddenly thoughtful, "are they crazy or are we? Have we been wrong all the time?"

Sarah, too, grew thoughtful. "I don't know, Tom."

"Why, we've been right, haven't we, Sarah?"

"I suppose so, Tom."

Sarah remembered that she was, above all, a sensible woman. And yet—surely she had heard what the wind said.

"Aren't you *sure*, Sarah?"

"Yes, Tom, of course."

There was silence for a moment.

"Sarah, you don't sound so sure."

"Well, Tom, perhaps I'm not, after all."

"Do you think we *are* a little crazy?"

"Oh, Tom, I don't know." And she didn't. Perhaps they were right, perhaps wrong; likelier wrong, and yet she'd rather be right. Why did Tom keep asking such questions?

"Look, Sarah, the way to be sure is to go to the window now and listen. Come with me."

She went willingly with him, and they stood a long time listening. At first she thought she heard a word or two in the wind's voice. Then she thought, and in a minute was sure, that she was hearing nothing but inarticulate sounds.

"I don't hear the wind saying anything, Tom."

The look on his face told her that he, too, had heard nothing.

"Oh, just a minute, Sarah. Perhaps . . . "

Again they listened, while the inarticulate wind wandered about outside.

"Perhaps what, Tom?"

There was a silence in which even the wind made no sound.

"I don't know, Sarah."

"Tom," Sarah said. "It was a beautiful dream we had together."

The cry of the wind had ceased, and the sound of the sea as it murmured seemed very far away.

Beneath Their Blue, Blue Skins

by John Forrester

When the warning came, Katherine Two Bears was on the bridge of the *Children's Starship*. She was only ten years old, eight years too young to be there. But she had been invited by her friend Ming Lo, who had told her to stand very quietly against the back wall and just observe.

Ming Lo was the navigator's assistant, and she knew they were coming into range of subspace signals from the Green Planet. She wanted Katherine to share the excitement. Their starship had been outbound from Earth for a whole year now, traveling toward the new world colony at underlight speed. And this would be their very first message from the colonists there.

Everyone on the bridge was quiet with expectation. The minutes were working by so slowly it almost seemed to hurt. Then suddenly there was a whine followed by static over the speakers.

"Starship of Children!" the panicky voice cried. *"Starship of Children, SOS! SOS! Warning! We're sealed in! The whole colony is trapped! Please get here and get us out, but be careful! We don't know—"*

That was all. The signal just shut off, with a little crackle of sound.

This was more than just bad news. If the colony was in danger, *sealed in,* as the message had put it, then the *Children's Starship* with its eight hundred passengers and crew was flying straight toward the same danger. And if the colony had perished by the time they arrived, then there would be no new home for these voyagers.

They all knew they could never go back to Earth again, either.

At certain points in their flight, they were able to accelerate and pass the speed of light, for just an instant. This meant huge time gains for them, but it also meant that the Earth they had known was now in their distant past. Even though they grew older at a normal rate, everyone left behind them had now passed into ancient history.

That was the strangest thing about space and time and light: When you went fast enough across the skin of space, you also shot forward in time. And your parents, your friends, your whole childhood world— all of it vanished into time past.

So if they couldn't land and settle on the Green Planet, in the star system Baltax-3, they would be sentenced to wandering in the darkness of space until their supplies were exhausted. And then the *Children's Starship* would become a floating tomb.

Finally Captain Moughrabi found his deep voice, and the first thing he focused on was Katherine Two Bears.

"Who let that child in here?" he yelled, glaring at Ming Lo.

"I did, sir," she said.

"Well, you take her out! And this goes on your record!"

"Yes, sir," Ming Lo said, taking Katherine's hand and hurrying into the elevator.

When the doors closed, Katherine threw her arms around Ming Lo. "I'm sorry!" she cried. "I didn't mean to get you in trouble!"

"Shh, shh, shh," Ming Lo said softly, smoothing back Katherine's long, black hair. "It's all right, you didn't do anything. He's just upset."

"So am I!" Katherine said, looking up at Ming Lo. "So are you! He didn't have to yell at you like that!"

"I know. Listen, this message . . . it's not for the children. Not yet, anyway. Do you understand?"

"I think so."

"You mustn't tell a soul, Katherine. Promise me."

"Okay. But the captain will tell them *eventually,* won't he?"

"Of course. But the right time is for the Board to decide, not for you or me. Understand?"

"Yes."

"Good. For now, this is between us. *Promise?"*

Katherine Two Bears nodded.

The elevator came to a stop and opened on the gymnasium level.

"Katherine!" her friends cried. "We're going to swim now! Come with us!"

She looked back at Ming Lo for just a second, and the promise to keep the secret was in her eyes.

* * *

But the Board decided against frightening the passengers and crew members, so they were never told.

Months slipped past, and then years. Katherine turned fourteen, and Ming Lo twenty-five. The uneasy secret lay between them, never spoken of. Katherine waited and waited, knowing her friend would tell her anything she could.

They swam together in the big pool, ran laps on the gym's track, and sunbathed beneath the heat lamps in the exercise room. But they never talked about that subspace warning. And Katherine never visited the bridge again. She was terrified of Captain Moughrabi and always carefully avoided him in the corridors.

"I have some news," Ming Lo said one day as they lay beneath the lamps. White towels were folded over their eyes, and they had the corner section to themselves.

"Hmmmm?"

"You understand the theory of underlight speed, don't you?"

"Sure. Sort of. We're going just a fraction beneath the speed of light, aren't we? And at certain intervals we actually go *above* that speed, for the briefest time?"

"Yes. Lightskips, they're called."

"I know."

"Well, what you don't know is that the science team has decided that we can make an extra lightskip on this journey—it'll be safe."

"Really? That means we'll get there quicker, doesn't it?"

"A *lot* quicker."

"Let's see," Katherine said, "we're supposed to arrive at the planet just as I turn sixteen . . ."

"Yes, but now you'll be much younger."

Katherine sat up and let her towel fall. She squinted against the glaring lights, and then she lay on her side and watched her friend.

"How young?"

Ming Lo spoke without changing her tone of voice. "Captain Moughrabi will announce it tonight," she said. "We'll be entering planetary orbit in one month."

Katherine caught her breath. A month! Ming Lo adjusted her own eyes to the light and grinned. When their eyes met, Katherine felt how much Ming Lo was worrying. There had been no more messages from the colony. Katherine didn't have to ask.

Ming Lo was tall and willowy graceful. Her long face was kind and always trying to break into a smile.

Katherine had the broad face and body of her Miccosukee Seminole ancestors. Her hair was as black as her friend's, and her dark eyes were only a little less slanted. She was considered a beauty on the starship.

One month. Katherine couldn't believe it. But what

if the colony was already destroyed? That night she had a very hard time going to sleep. And that was the night the blue dreams began.

* * *

Blue surfaces, vast and tight, slid through waves of foamy water. Katherine was at sea, drifting freely among whales. Then she saw tall, blue shapes among dense trees, and she was in a mountain forest. The shadows were very deep, and there was a smell of nutmeg and bananas. The blue forms were moving gracefully in thickets of green cane and high fern.

When the singing began, Katherine barely breathed. It was the most beautiful song she had ever imagined. It rose from one of the huge, blue forms in the cool shadows, floated through the woods like smoke, and only stopped as another of the creatures took it up. Each of them had a slightly different voice—one more like a pleading flute, another reminding her of a mourning violin. But what music! Katherine felt it penetrate her whole body, drawing her into the circle of half-hidden, blue beings all around her.

She sat up in bed.

The dream was still with her for a moment, and as it faded she reached out with both arms to bring it back. But as the full awareness that it was a dream slowly came over her, she lay back down and began to cry. Why did she want those blue beings, and their sad, compelling songs, so desperately?

The next night, the dreams came again. Only this time she was in clear, windswept snowfields, high in peaks of mountains. The blue ones called from caves just above her, casting their long shadows on the icy snow. She tried to go to them, but her feet broke through the crust, and she sank down hopelessly into the white world. And in the distance, those tragic voices began to sing.

In the morning, her hands were bluish when she woke up. She ran to wash them, and then hesitated, holding them up to the light. She was afraid it *would* wash away. And then, before her eyes, the color faded.

She ran to find Ming Lo and tell her about the dreams.

Her friend listened carefully as they walked together in the ship's botanical gardens. Here it was cool and moist, and they loved to breathe the clean fresh air of the plants.

"It was a place like this, in one of the dreams," Katherine told her. "And they were all through there." She pointed into the density of giant figs wound in vines. At their feet clusters of orchids bloomed.

"What could it mean, Ming Lo?" she asked.

"It has something to do with the Green Planet," Ming Lo said.

"Really? How do you know?"

"Because we've been receiving similar images on the light scrambler."

"*What?*"

"Yes. We know that planet is full of big creatures of some kind, Katherine. The strange thing is, we can't pick up any signs of the colony."

Katherine was silent.

"Look," Ming Lo said, "I'm not supposed to tell you this, but in the original pictures from the Green Planet, our scientists found a lot of new species there. It appeared that none of them had our kind of intelligence. That's one reason they decided to colonize. The things you're sensing are the planet's largest living beings, and they seem most like dinosaurs—in the images."

"Or whales?"

"Yes! Some of them live in the Green Planet's oceans. But they aren't intelligent, so they can't be our problem. Besides, the colonists are very well armed."

Katherine's stomach was beginning to hurt.

"I thought they weren't supposed to carry guns into space."

"Well, they weren't!" Ming Lo's lips were trembling. "And I wasn't supposed to tell you that."

"But they did anyway? How could they be allowed?"

"The people planning the expeditions . . . " Ming Lo said desperately, ". . . they decided . . . by the time we reach the Green Planet . . . Earth won't even *exist*! You realize that, don't you?"

"So the laws don't matter?"

"That's what they thought. And the planners, they told Captain Moughrabi he'd better take them, he might need them. Oh, Katherine, you *mustn't* tell on me!"

"But the people on Earth were told we don't have any weapons?"

"That's right. *Say* you won't repeat this. Not to anyone."

"No . . . no." Katherine's whole middle was aching.

"How did you find out?"

"Everybody who works on the bridge knows."

"Oh. Listen, Ming Lo, something's the matter with me," Katherine said. "I've got to go lie down, okay?"

"Sure, of course." Ming Lo put her arm around Katherine and helped her down the hallway.

When they reached Katherine's room Ming Lo tucked her in.

"I'll be back to check on you," she said.

Katherine nodded.

"Remember not to tell on me, about the weapons, okay?"

Katherine kept nodding and held her stomach. The whole room was beginning to turn blue.

* * *

She was dreaming the rich, blue songs when they shook her awake.

"Katherine! *Katherine!*" Ming Lo cried.

She felt drugged, saw them through haze, heard their voices ringing and ringing around her.

"Come back!" Ming Lo cried. *"Stay with us!"*

Then Katherine's head hurt sharply, and the lights of the room were bright and harsh. She shut her eyes and whispered, "I'm here. Just give me a minute, please."

When she opened her eyes and adjusted to the light, she saw a room full of worried faces. There were Ming Lo and stern-faced Captain Moughrabi, and the whole science team was surrounding her bed.

"Are you okay?" Ming Lo asked.

She nodded.

"Listen," her friend said. "Each time you sleep, you go farther away from us. They're after you, Katherine. They're *taking* you."

"Who is?"

Ming Lo shook her long arms. "The blue creatures. On the planet. Who else?"

"Oh. Yes."

"Pay attention. Science Officer Percy has some things to say."

Science Officer Roberta Percy was a small black woman who talked so fast it made Katherine nervous. But with all these intense eyes trained on her, she listened as carefully as she could.

"Katherine," Officer Percy said, "you know that each of us was chosen from thousands of others who wanted to make this voyage, don't you?"

"Yes."

"Earth can only last a little longer, perhaps a few decades. And then the Visiting Star—which is hurtling toward her at a million miles a second—will be within gravitational range. The orbits of our solar system will be warped and skewed—and Earth will be dragged away from the warmth of the sun."

"It's already happened," Katherine said sadly.

"You mean because of our speed?"

"Yes."

"We mustn't think that way! The point is, Earth doesn't have long, and those who have been selected for these colonizing voyages have a special responsibility."

"I know that."

"And you understand that every person on board has something special to contribute to the mission?"

"Of course." Katherine was beginning to be really alert now.

"You were chosen because of your empathic abilities, were you not?"

"Yes."

"You have the power to read our minds, do you not?"

"No, not exactly, Officer. I can read *feelings*. Sometimes a few thoughts. But mostly just feelings."

"Ah, yes. And we have never called on you before, have we? Because we haven't needed this curious ability. But now, you are somehow in tune with the creatures on the planet's surface."

"It seems so."

"And what are they feeling?"

"Well . . . I don't know, exactly."

"Yes you do. Just relax, and ask yourself, on a gut level . . . What are they feeling?"

Katherine hesitated. Could she be right? There was only one theme to all the songs and all the images.

"Sadness," Katherine said. "They sing the most beautiful and the most heartbreaking songs there are."

"Always?" Officer Percy asked.

"Yes. The songs are different, but the feeling of them is always the same. And . . ."

"Yes?" The room full of faces drew closer to her.

"Complexity," she said. "The songs are more complicated than Earth music. Or any that I ever heard."

Captain Moughrabi straightened up at that. "Indeed," he said, as if he didn't believe it.

* * *

The next time Katherine slept she really joined them. The blueness of their skins became a warm, living substance that enveloped her, and the aching beauty of their songs held her in its satisfying trance. She could hear Ming Lo's voice from time to time, and she even managed to answer some of her questions, but Katherine couldn't wake up again. And down within her dream, when she thought of this problem, she smiled. Because she knew that she didn't want to wake up again.

Inside her dream, Katherine relived all her early years, remembering things that had happened when she was only two in exquisite brightness and clarity. She had grown up in the heart of the Everglades and been raised by her grandmother there. Louise Snow was a medicine woman, and she had known of Katherine's abilities before anyone else. It was she who had brought Katherine out of the swamps in her own canoe and delivered her on the steps of the special school for starship children. Katherine had been seven then.

That last night before they left the Everglades island, they had sat before the fire in Louise's camp.

"Child," her grandmother had said, "who are your true relatives?"

"All the animal persons," Katherine had replied very seriously.

"That's right. And what is our clan?"

"The panther."

"Yes. I feel a great destiny for you, Katherine. You will be chosen for this great trip to the new planet. Even if a million children ask to go, child, I know you will be chosen."

Katherine simply believed what her grandmother said.

"But you must never forget the Miccosukee people. And you mustn't forget this old woman, either."

Katherine sat closer to her grandmother on the big log. Out in the darkness of the swamp an alligator roared, and an owl replied in its mellow cackle.

"I'll never forget," she said.

"My grandfather was the friend of the deer. Whenever the people needed meat, he would rise in the morning and go out. Just go out of his camp a little way and sit down. Then a deer would come to him."

"And he would shoot it?"

"Yes. But first he would thank the deer for its life. The deer's life was its Giveaway. He gave it freely, to keep the people living. And in return, the people always treated deer with respect. They never killed one unless it was needed."

"The way the white men do?"

"That's right. They shoot them for what they call sport."

"Tell me about how *we* did it."

"Yes. Well, after your great-great-grandfather killed a deer, he performed a ceremony. He smoked a little sage, and then gave thanks to the deer's spirit, and to the spirits of the Sky Deer. After all that was done the right way, he would dress it, and take it to his people. That was *his* Giveaway. And when you're old enough, you'll know what your own Giveaway must be."

Katherine held her grandmother's soft hand.

"That friendship with the deer—it's in our family. It's in our blood, Katherine. And the other animals feel it, too. That's why you always know where they are."

Katherine smiled in the firelight. Ever since she'd been old enough to point her finger, she'd been able to tell where a deer was hiding, or a bear was feeding.

"I think this gift is what you must bring to the new world, Katherine. Can you remember my words?"

Katherine nodded very seriously.

"I have taught you a lot," her grandmother said. "But the most important things are in your blood."

*   *   *

The month passed, and the *Children's Starship* swung into planetary orbit around the Green Planet.

The ship's sensors located the colony settlement, and they picked up faint signs of life there. But the whole area was covered over by a mysterious dome. The science team determined that the planet was crawling—as they put it—with large blue creatures.

"But they can't be the cause of any trouble," Officer Percy said in her final report to the captain, "because they only have flippers or paws. Research shows that all intelligent creatures, all truly *dangerous* creatures, have finely developed hands. Hands are the first step toward technology and the development of real brains."

But Captain Moughrabi wasn't so sure. "Research shows, eh?" he said in a mocking tone.

He had Katherine brought to the bridge on her bed. She still lay in a trance sleep, dreaming deeply, but now she could answer Ming Lo's questions. And her replies were very clear.

"The colonists are all alive," she said, "inside the crystal dome."

"And what is this crystal dome?" Ming Lo asked.

"I must touch it," Katherine said. "Then I will know."

"That's out of the question," Officer Percy said.

They all watched as her skin pulsed pale, glowing blue.

Captain Moughrabi smiled slightly. "What have we got to lose?" he said.

Ming Lo straightened up and flushed.

"Sir—" Officer Percy began.

"Nothing!" the captain thundered. "We've got *nothing* to lose! She's not doing us any good up here, is she? And we've got to understand this before we attempt to land!"

"Sir," Ming Lo said in a trembling, furious voice, "isn't it against regulations to—"

"Shhhhh!" he replied, holding up his open palm to her. "Whatever this mission requires is what it will get."

"This is just a goose chase, anyway," Officer Percy said. "Those creatures *can't* be the problem! They simply don't have the intelligence."

"We don't absolutely know that," Captain Moughrabi said.

"There's nothing beneath those blue skins that we have to worry about," Officer Percy said. "Nothing but animal nerves, animal brains."

The captain turned to Ming Lo. "Will you go with her?" he asked.

"Of course," Ming Lo said. "Anywhere."

*   *   *

Katherine was hardly aware of being strapped into the cruiser beside Ming Lo. The starship's computer autopiloted them to within twenty miles of the colony, and Ming Lo took the wheel from there.

She made a smooth landing in a grassy marsh near the crystal dome.

And when she turned to look at Katherine, her friend was smiling, awake. Katherine released her own chair straps and opened her hatch.

She climbed down and stretched and breathed deeply.

"Does it feel good to be moving again?" Ming Lo asked.

But Katherine said in a strange, droning voice, "Come with me."

Ming Lo grabbed the communicator and hurried after

her. Katherine was surprisingly fast as she moved through the tall grasses and over the wet earth.

Ming Lo felt as if she were following a wild deer.

But Ming Lo stopped when she saw the creatures coming. From across the marsh, from out of the dark woods, the blue giants were moving. They were as tall as buildings, harmless looking, waddly, but somehow graceful as well. They were like dinosaurs, with soft-looking ridges down their backs. And even from this distance, there was something about their movements and their eyes.

Ming Lo knew inside that Officer Percy had been wrong. These were not beasts, as Earth had used that word.

And there were so many of them! Ming Lo's heart was flying. She contacted the ship and told them what she saw.

And Katherine walked on. In a moment she was standing beside the great, crystal structure that arched over the former colony. Through its translucent wall she could have seen the desperate, pleading settlers, as they jumped up and down and banged on the inside of their perfect prison. She could have seen them if she had turned her head, but she had no need to look. She could feel it all.

"We're here," they cried, their voices faintly penetrating the crystal. *"Look at us! We're here!"*

But Katherine Two Bears kept her eyes on the great blue ones.

As they waddled closer and closer to her, she saw

vivid scenes of the Earth-colonists' landing, of the friendship offerings the blue beings had made. There were great piles of turniplike roots, of sweet leaves and spices, and finally of salad-flowers, all spread before the landing site.

And Katherine saw the colonists laughing, unpacking their rifles and lasers.

They were making jokes about how blue monsters might taste.

And the blue ones had sensed it, had felt it, and a tremor had started to ripple back through them, passing from nerve to nerve over thousands of them. It had crossed the mountains and traveled into the oceans, penetrating the great swimming herds of blue water beings, cousins and feeling-kin to the land-living ones.

All this Katherine felt as she stood beside the dome, and as she heard the Earthlings begging and crying and pounding for her to turn.

"Can't you hear us?" they screamed. *"What have they done to you? Radio your ship! Have them blast these dragons off the face of the planet!"*

As she held out her hands, the great ones came forward, forming a circle, almost touching her.

She could visualize the colonists shooting them by dozens.

She saw grinning men examining the thick, electric-blue skin. It didn't seem to fade like the skin of a dead thing. She saw them slicing it into patterns for shoes and shirts and capes. And she smelled the fire and thick smoke as the Earthlings barbecued great hunks of the blue ones' flesh.

It was against Earth's laws, to kill new species. But those were only laws for the public back home. And that public, of course, was gone forever. *It's only in our memories now*, she thought.

Katherine felt the confusion and pain of the blue beings as they shrank from their assassins. In her mind, she saw them hiding in their thickest forest and calling a council. But the Earthling hunters kept coming. Now they were stalking the blue ones for sport. They were shooting them just to see them fall.

Suddenly Katherine knew that the blue beings had spun the crystal dome from their own bodies, from a substance they did not think about, but which came easily as they needed it. There were tiny holes in the dome for air, and Katherine knew, also, that a small opening appeared in the crystal surface when the blue ones wanted it, for their offerings of grasses and leaves and the cleanest water. Their prisoners would live out their lives in good health.

The blue beings were so near her now, crowds of them, fat and sleek, touching each other's smooth bodies. But they never shoved. Katherine could feel their incredible politeness toward each other.

She raised her arms, and Ming Lo saw that she was as blue as they were.

Ming Lo ran toward her, clutching the ship's communicator with both hands. The communicator was her

one link to all those human souls circling above, and
to the chance that Katherine carried. For what? Ming
Lo wondered as she ran. For everything! It has to be!
For peace with these creatures! And forgiveness for
whatever our people have done!

She reached Katherine and she felt the warmth of
those great, luminous bodies, and she smelled their
strong scents of nutmeg and bananas.

"*Katherine Two Bears!*" Ming Lo cried. "*I am your
friend! I call on you to help me save our people!*"

Ming Lo held the communicator toward Katherine,
with the channel to the bridge open. "*You're the only
chance we've got, Katherine,*" she said. "*Remember
who you are.*"

Katherine reached with both hands open, and the
communicator floated slowly from Ming Lo to her. She
knelt down and gently touched its sides. A film of fine,
translucent crystal began to grow around it.

"*Katherine! No!* You're a *person*! Think of *us*!"

Katherine stood up and smiled.

"My grandmother sent me to this world," she said.
"I realize that now."

"*No!*" Ming Lo pleaded. "You're part of the *Children's Starship* mission! *That's* why you're here—to
begin the new colony!"

"Colony . . ." Katherine said. "Grandmother Snow
always hated that word."

"Please," Ming Lo said. "Please."

"I know I'm part of the mission," Katherine said.

"But I'm also part of all my relatives. And that means all the animal persons, Ming Lo."

"Katherine, if you don't help us, we'll die."

They both looked down at the crystal globe that completely surrounded the communicator.

"Go back to the starship," Katherine said. "Tell them to return in one year. If there is a way to live in peace, perhaps we will all have found it by then."

"A year!"

"Go on, Ming Lo. The people inside the dome will be all right. And so will you."

"But—"

"Ming Lo, I'm only telling you what I feel. By the time a year passes, I'll have entered the Council of the Blue Ones. They're already calling me there now."

Ming Lo stood in the breeze of the field, trying to find words.

But there were no more.

"When you return," Katherine said, "make sure that all the weapons have been cast out into space. Everything. From the laser cannon down to the hand weapons they're hiding."

"Yes, all right."

"I will know," Katherine said. "Tell them that."

"Good-bye," Ming Lo said sadly.

"Wait," Katherine said. "Tell them this, also. I have not been 'taken over' by anyone. I am empathic—they know that—but I am also a Miccosukee of the Panther Clan. And my great-great-grandfather was brother to the deer. Tell them . . . I will be the voice that speaks for these creatures . . . and for this Green Planet."

"All right," Ming Lo said. She was already walking away, her head down.

When she was a hundred yards across the windy marsh, she turned back for a final look, and Katherine was still watching her. Katherine waved, and it seemed, perhaps, that she also smiled.

Inside the crystal dome, the colonists had stopped their hoarse yelling and their helpless pounding. They stared at Katherine as she rose high into the air, riding just behind the ears of a great one.

And from a thousand blue beings at once, the singing began.

Bear at the Gate

by Jessica Amanda Salmonson

The little teddy bear was surprised to find himself whole. He had both his button eyes, all his limbs, and felt well stuffed with sawdust. He stood before an enormous gate, gazing up. Around him drifted clouds. The staircase shined of pearl.

The gate opened and a winged man looked out. "Who is this little fellow?" asked St. Peter.

"I'm Henry," said the bear.

St. Peter went away for a moment, then returned with a book, running a delicate finger down the list.

"Just Henry?" he asked.

"Yes."

"Well, there's no Henry listed here. I'm not certain you can enter."

"Enter where?" asked Henry. "I'm not sure I'd want to, really. What's it like?"

"It's not perfect," said St. Peter. "But it's paradise."

"Oh, I think I understand," said Henry, suddenly aware. "I must be dead and this is Heaven. I thought it was odd that I had all my limbs back."

"Hmmm." Peter was thinking. "It's highly irregular to get a stuffed toy at the gate; but clearly yours is an authentic soul. Not all toys have souls, you understand. How did you come to die?"

"Torn limb from limb by an impish boy," said Henry. "Alas! I was an antique bear and had been well cared for, although I lost my eye early on. . . ." (Here he felt upward with his paw, still surprised to have both eyes.) "I hadn't been played with for a long time but had remained stored away in a secret place so that the Old Man could take me out from time to time and look at me. When the Old Man died, most of his stuff was thrown away; it wasn't worth much. As for me, the Old Man's daughter and son-in-law tossed me to the Old Man's grandson, like an old rag tossed to a dog. I think he rather liked me a bit; but he had a funny way of showing it. He tore my arms off and stabbed me with a jackknife, and my sawdust spilled out on the floor."

"Hmmm," said St. Peter once again. "That was an unfortunate end. Yet nothing in your story explains how you came to sprout a soul."

"I'm sure I never knew I had one," said Henry.

"Well, tell me how you lived—before you were stored away, that is."

"Oh, I had a grand time. When the Old Man was a toddler, he got me for Christmas. He wasn't much bigger than me and crawled more than he walked. He dragged me around with him. I lost my eye before New Year's, but the sensitive child was so alarmed that he was awfully careful after that and treated me terribly well. When he was about sixteen he decided he was a bit old for a teddy bear and put me on a high shelf. When he got married he put me in a box. When be became a widower, he put the box in the attic. I'd gotten tattered over the years and had a few patches, but I was still a stout little fellow." He looked himself up and down, finding no evidence of the wear and tear or the scars of repair.

Still, Peter saw no excuse for a soul, and asked, "Tell me your three strongest memories," for this was a sure test.

Henry wrinkled up his brow and said: "My earliest memory is of that Christmas when I first got hugged. That was awfully nice."

"And your second strongest memory?"

"When I first got put away. That was awfully sad."

"And in between?"

Henry acted as though he didn't want to say.

"What is it?" Peter urged, still standing in the gate, his huge wings spreading out behind.

"It was when the Old Man was eight."

"And?"

"He got sick."

Henry was *very* reluctant to say more.

"You felt bad about that?" said Peter.

"Very bad. He had a terrible fever, and he died."

"He died?" Peter raised a brow. "Then how did he come to be the Old Man?"

"Well, you see, his fever was awful, and he started imagining things. He imagined I was alive and walking around. 'Dearest Henry,' he said to me, 'my throat is so dry, and I need a glass of water.' He was very pitiful, and I just had to get him a glass of water, only I couldn't. Later on he said, 'Dearest Henry, I don't feel nice.' And that's when I found the strength to put my paws around his neck and nuzzle his face just so. I could feel the pulse through the vein of his neck. I felt it stop entirely, and I knew he was dead. 'Do come back,' I whispered. 'Do come back.' And as I said it in his ear very softly, his pulse began anew, the fever broke, and he got better."

"My," said St. Peter. "That was wonderful of you to care so much. Obviously that is how you gained your soul, and that is why you're here at this gate. Still, it is *highly* irregular. There aren't many toys walking around in here. . . . Oh, just a minute."

St. Peter went away again, leaving the gate ajar. Henry heard someone talking to St. Peter, and St. Peter whispering back. Then the gate began to open all the way. There stood a little boy with shining, happy eyes. "Old Man!" cried Henry, and ran into the young boy's arms. "Henry!" said the Old Man, and carried the bear into paradise.

St. Peter shrugged his wings and shoulders, then closed the gate.

What Are You Going to Be When You Grow Up?

by Gregory Benford

At dinner his sister asked the question that had been bothering Mark all day.

"What are *you* going to be when you grow up, Mark?" Claire asked. She had been talking all through dinner about Jobs Week at their school. It was a series of films and talks about what adults did at work. All Mark's friends had been talking about it too.

"I don't know," Mark said irritably. "Maybe a cowboy."

Claire laughed along with Mark's father and mother. "There aren't cowboys anymore," she said.

"Sure there are!" Mark said. "On TV."

"Those are actors," his father said quietly.

Mark had been feeling more and more uncomfortable all week. All his friends at school seemed to know what they were going to be as adults. But until Jobs Week started, Mark hadn't even thought about having to hold a job. It suddenly seemed as though he was far behind everybody else.

"Well," he said, searching for something to say, "I like developing pictures in Photography Club."

"Machines develop film now," Claire said haughtily. "I saw some on a field trip." She was two years older than Mark and liked to remind everybody.

Mark pressed his lips together and decided not to get into an argument with his sister. It never paid off. "Dad," he said, "what's your job like?"

His father looked startled. Usually his father never talked about work while he was at home. "I'm a scientist, and I do a lot of complicated things," he said vaguely.

"We *know* that, Daddy," Claire said. "You're impossibly brilliant, *every*body agrees."

They all laughed. Mark's father smiled and said, "I think about problems, mostly."

"Very *com*plicated problems," Claire said in a hollow, joking voice.

"Don't you use your hands?" Mark asked.

"Sure. Sometimes I build electronics instruments."

Mark considered this, nodding his head in approval. He liked the concrete feel of making things. Fixing them was good too. He enjoyed tinkering with the engines of his father's power tools. "Is it fun?"

"Why not come see?" his father asked.

"Could I?"

"I think it could be arranged," his father said, as he

spooned out some red sherbet dessert for them all. "I can show you my big surprise."

Mark had been thinking about what it would be like to fix cars, or maybe airplanes. "Huh? What, Dad?"

Mom said, "Your father has been working on a time machine."

Claire looked puzzled. "You mean a clock? There are lots of clocks already."

"No, dummy," Mark said. It felt good to call her a name, but his mother frowned at him, and Mark started again. "No, Claire. Clocks just *measure* time. A time machine lets you *travel* in time."

"Travel?" Claire raised her eyebrows.

"To go into the past," Mother explained. "Or into the future."

"You mean I could visit last week?" Claire asked, staring off into space with a vacant look.

"In a way," Dad said. He handed around dessert. There was a silence while everyone started eating.

Mark wanted to ask more questions. But after dessert there were dishes for him and Claire to do, and then homework. He decided to wait until tomorrow, when he could talk to his father alone. Then he could see the time machine itself.

* * *

Mark had visited his father's laboratory before, but somehow today it seemed different. For one thing, his father didn't just show him the offices in the front of the building. Instead, he took Mark back through the offices filled with clattering computer printers and people making big drawings. They pushed open a tall, heavy door. Beyond were the big, open rooms where the experiments were done. This was the heart of the laboratory.

There were rows of computers and electrical power devices. Thick wires—colored orange, or yellow, or red—seemed to wind their way all over the big rooms. Mark nearly tripped on one.

His father led him among humming machinery. Men and women were repairing complex electronics instruments. People peered at television screens that were filled with numbers and printing.

"Wow," Mark said, "making a time machine is a lot of work."

"Yes, it is," his father said. "And this is the very first time machine ever invented. We're still just learning how to use it."

"Dad, where *is* the time machine?"

"What?" His father looked around at Mark in surprise. "Why, all around us. Everything you see is part of the machine." He waved a hand to take in all the laboratory.

"I thought it would be something like . . . well . . . like a car."

"Maybe someday it will be, Mark. But for now— Come, I'll show you."

His father led Mark into a small room. Lights winked and flickered on one wall.

It looked interesting, but Mark couldn't help but

think that even time travel seemed a little dull. The laboratory was mostly gray cabinets and workbenches.

He had seen a television show about time travel once. The people in the show wore bright red uniforms. They went back in time to hunt dinosaurs with laser pistols. It was very exciting. Of course, Mark knew his father wasn't doing anything like that. But still . . .

"This is the heart of the time machine," Dad said.

"It looks like a telephone booth," Mark said.

And it did. Mark could see through the sides of the little booth. There was an ordinary wooden chair inside.

"Not very impressive," Mark said.

His father nodded. "I agree, it's not. But it works."

"How?"

"I'll show you."

Dad led him over to a small table near the booth. "Let me have your hand," he said.

Mark's father took his hand and stuck one finger into a tube. "Hold still." Mark felt the jab of a needle.

"What's that?" Mark said, startled.

"The tracer," Dad said. "It takes a little piece of your skin. A sample. Then it looks at the molecules in your body."

"It hurts," Mark said, taking his finger out of the tube. "Not much, though."

"The machine memorizes the special molecules you have in you. Your DNA molecules, we call them. Then it can find you in the future."

"Find me?"

"Yes, that's right." Dad looked at him. "There's a Mark in the future. He's not the same as you are now, of course. He's older, and different. But he has the same basic molecules in him that you do."

"So this machine finds him?"

"That's it. The time machine can take you into the future—*your* future. Not your body, though. Just your, well, a piece of your mind."

"What piece?"

"Well, suppose you went into the future. You would see things as though you were the Mark at that time. The future Mark."

"Oh . . . " Mark studied the booth, thinking.

"The machine follows what we call your space-time track. That's the path you follow both in space and in time. The machine finds you in the future. And *only* you. That way, you can't interfere with anybody else's future."

"I see," said Mark. He was beginning to think of a plan.

"Say—" Dad glanced at his watch. "Time waits for no man, as the poet said. I have to check on some things."

"I'll wait here, Dad."

"Good. I'll be right back."

"See you, Dad."

When the door closed Mark suddenly felt very alone. He had thought of an idea, and if he dared . . .

Mark studied the dials and switches beside the booth.

Above two of the dials was printed FUTURE DATE.

Each dial was like a clock. One was marked with years. Mark used a knob beside the clock to set it for fifteen years in the future.

The other clocklike dial showed months. Mark set it for October. He had always liked the fall.

Without giving himself time to think about his plan, he stepped into the booth and closed the door. It clicked shut.

The booth was completely quiet. There were buttons on the booth's wall.

A light winked on red. Then it turned green.

Mark sat down and studied the control panel inside the booth. There was another dial like a clock. Under it was printed LENGTH OF TRIP.

Mark turned the knob beside the clock until it read 45 MINUTES. That seemed like long enough to visit the future.

The clock buzzed.

Suddenly a tiny television screen on the control panel flickered into life. A word flashed onto the screen: READY.

The booth hummed. Mark looked out at the laboratory clock on the far wall. It read 4:36 P.M.

The humming got louder. The lights dimmed.

Well, Mark thought, *if I want to find out what I'll be when I grow up, this is the way to do it.*

He clenched his teeth.

Something screeched. The lights went out.

Pop.

*   *   *

Pop.

The laboratory was gone.

The booth was gone.

Mark looked around. He was standing in a big, cold room. A steady *bang bang bang* came from nearby.

He turned. A man in a cap was hammering on the front of a car. The car was bent and broken in several places. It must have been in a wreck. *Bang clang crash.*

"Hey!" The man in a cap looked up at Mark. "Come here and hold this for me."

Mark walked over. There were other cars here. Men were working on them. He tripped over a rubber car tire lying on the concrete floor.

"Come on!" the man called out. Mark hurried.

"Here." The man pointed at the front of the car. "Hold it."

The car had a kind of grill on its front. Mark had never seen anything like it. He bent over and held the metal grill at the edge, away from the big dent in the center.

The man frowned. "No, higher." Mark put his hands further up. "Okay."

The man adjusted his cap and began hitting the grill. He used a big hammer that had a rubber head on it. *Bang bang clang.* The noise hurt Mark's ears.

He gritted his teeth and looked at the car. It was small and funny-shaped. The back was narrow and it didn't stand very high off the floor. The car looked hard to get into. Suddenly Mark realized that this was the way cars would look fifteen years from his time. He couldn't tell if this one was better than the cars he was used to, but it certainly *looked* uncomfortable.

Bang clang. The man stopped. The dent was straight now.

He noticed the way Mark was studying the car. "Some baby, huh?" he asked.

"What?" Mark said.

"Some fancy car, isn't it? Costs a lot."

"This?" Mark was surprised.

"Why, sure." The man looked at Mark. "It'll be a long time before you or I can afford to buy one of these jobs."

"Oh. I see." He didn't really see at all, but Mark nodded anyway. He stood up. He felt an ache in his back.

Now that he thought about it, his body seemed different. Mark looked down. His blue coveralls could not hide the bulging muscles in his arms and legs.

He was a *man.* He brought up a big hand and stared at the thick ridges of callus on it. Mark felt his cheek. A light beard rasped against his fingers. It felt so strange to be grown up. . . .

Mark walked over to a grimy window. His body felt heavier and more solid than when he had been a boy.

Rain spattered on the window. This didn't look like a very pretty part of town. He could make out a gray factory across the street. A short truck rumbled by.

It had a strange machine with funny arms and levers riding in the back.

Mark moved over to the next window. His boots made a *clump clump* sound. When he peered out the window he had to blink twice to be sure he was seeing things correctly.

A crew of workers were fixing part of the street. They were digging a hole. Some others were mixing black, sticky tar in a big bucket. But the repairmen weren't men at all—they were chimpanzees!

The chimpanzees wore yellow uniforms with long sleeves. A man worked with them, showing them what to do. The chimpanzees could shovel dirt out of the hole very fast. They carried buckets of tar—far more than a man could.

Somehow these chimpanzees looked different from the ones Mark had seen in the zoo. They tilted back their furry heads and listened when the man spoke to them. Could they understand English?

Mark wondered if something had been done to the chimpanzees to make them smarter. They looked so odd, all bent over and digging with their long arms. . . .

"Hey! Mark! Get back to work!"

Mark looked around to see who had shouted at him. A short man had an angry expression on his face and was pointing at a repair bench nearby.

"No time to daydream, lookin' out the window," the man yelled harshly.

Mark nodded. He sat down at the workbench. Somehow he knew which tools to pick out and what to do with them. He took a socket wrench over to the nearest car and opened the car's hood. He remembered that he was supposed to fix the engine.

Mark worked steadily for several minutes. It was hard to concentrate with all the noise in the garage. His feet were cold. He stamped them on the concrete to warm them.

Still, it felt good to have a job to do, and to know how to do it. There was something fun about taking an engine that didn't work and making it run again.

Mark felt a bit strange in this older body. He could remember, in the back of his mind, other things about his job. He had done these same repairs earlier in the day, and in the days before, too.

One part of him was bored because he had repeated this same job so many times before, on other cars. But another part of him liked the feel of doing it, of putting things right.

Mark shook his head. It was confusing. Did he like this work, or not? He wasn't sure.

He reached for a screwdriver and wiped his brow. Then the clatter of the garage work began to fade. He looked up. The lights were getting pale.

Pop.

Pop.

Stillness.

Mark opened his eyes. Neon light came flooding in. He was back in the booth.

He looked at the clock on the far wall. It read 4:36 P.M.

Mark blinked. He had spent forty-five minutes in the future. But the time machine had returned him to exactly the moment when he left!

Quickly he stepped out of the booth and clicked the door shut. His head was swimming with all the things that he'd seen, but Mark wanted to be sure he didn't get caught using the machine. His father was sure to be angry.

Mark returned all the dials on the front of the booth to where they had been before his trip. He spun the last one into place with a clicking sound. Behind him he could hear a door open.

"Well," his father said, "anything more you want to see?"

Mark held his breath, thinking of all the things he had seen in the last forty-five minutes. Then he said, "No, not really, Dad."

Mark's father looked at his wrist watch. "Almost five o'clock. Let's go home early. Time flies by, doesn't it?"

"Yes," said Mark. "Time flies."

*   *   *

On the bus going home Dad talked about the laboratory. Mark tried to listen, but he couldn't. He kept trying to figure out everything that had happened in the future.

He was going to become a garage mechanic, that was clear. It had been fun part of the time too. But other parts weren't fun. Did he really want to spend all his life in that garage?

"Dad," Mark said over the rumble of the bus, "people have used your time machine, haven't they?"

"Of course," his father answered. "A few have gone into the future so far—*their* futures, I mean."

"So they know how their lives are going to turn out?"

"No, not exactly."

"Why not?"

"Well, they saw what will happen *if* they keep on the way they are. That is, keep doing the things they already are doing."

"Then the future really isn't the way they saw it?" Mark asked.

"Well . . ." Mark's father wrinkled his brow, thinking. "What they saw is something we call a probability set."

"What's that?"

"Well, Mark, let's say *you* had gone into the future. Your future."

"Okay." Mark smiled a little. Did Dad suspect?

"Then you saw what will become of you. If you liked what you saw, fine. Just keep on doing what you were doing already, and your future will turn out the way you saw it."

"What if I didn't like it?"

"Ummm . . . " Mark's father frowned again and rubbed his jaw. "Then I guess you could change things. Stop doing what you were doing. We haven't tried anything like that using the machine yet, though."

Dad looked at Mark as their bus slowed at their stop. "That's a very interesting question, Mark. Asking the right questions is the most important part of science. Maybe you should be a scientist."

"Maybe so," Mark said. "Come on, Dad, let's get home. I've got to help make supper."

*　*　*

At supper that evening Claire talked a lot about her friends. They were all interested in playing football on the school team. The girls had a team as well as the boys.

"Why you spend your time on that photography stuff I'll never know, Mark," Claire said. "Not when you could be playing football. You used to be good at it."

She leaned forward, expecting an argument. Mark and Claire nearly always disagreed about something over supper. They enjoyed the chance to match wits.

But tonight Mark said simply, "Maybe you're right," and kept on eating his supper.

For a moment Claire was speechless. Then she said, "You mean you'll start going to the football tryouts every afternoon?"

"Yes," Mark said, and kept eating.

Dad looked at Mark and smiled. "That sounds like a good idea. You can get outside and have some exercise."

"That's not why I'm doing it, though, Dad," Mark said.

"Well then," Mark's mother said warmly, "why are you? You'll have to give up the Photography Club for football."

"I know," Mark said. "But I've been thinking. I'd like to play football for one of the big teams."

"You mean play on the school team when you get to high school?" Claire asked.

"No. A *professional* team."

"You mean the ones on television?" Dad asked.

"Yes."

They all looked at Mark, surprised.

"That's *hard*," Claire said. "Really, Mark, you have no idea how hard. It's *impossible*."

"Claire, it isn't impossible," Mom said. "But it is difficult." She looked at Mark, concerned. "You know, dear, I don't want you to get hurt. Football is a rough game."

"Then I suppose I had better find out if I can take it," Mark said seriously.

"It seems awfully ambitious," Mom said slowly.

"I think we have an ambitious son," Dad said. Dad glanced at Mom, and Mark could see him give her a wink.

* * *

For the next two months Mark's world was football, and only football. He practiced each school day. He met friends for games in a vacant lot on Saturday and Sunday afternoons. He read books about football tactics. In his dreams he would see himself carrying the ball down the field, puffing as he ran over the green grass, the crowd cheering. Or else he was the one who threw the ball for a winning touchdown.

At supper he talked about football constantly. He asked Dad what position he should play.

"Play whatever your coach says," Mark's father answered.

Mark nodded. He knew his father was right. The coach knew best. But deep inside, Mark wanted to be the quarterback. That way he would get to throw the passes. There was something about seeing the ball fly through the air and land in exactly the right spot that thrilled Mark. He couldn't put it into words, but he knew that was what he wanted to do.

One afternoon, after practice, Mark's friend Anna was watching as he came off the field. She held a camera.

Mark's football cleats rasped against the concrete walkway as he stopped beside her. He rubbed a sore leg muscle.

"You're getting to be a good player, Mark," she said. "I was watching."

"I'm okay," Mark said. "Getting better."

"Your sister, Claire, told me you want to be a football player when you grow up," Anna said.

"Not *want* to be. *Will* be," Mark said.

"You've changed, Mark," Anna said.

"Oh? How?"

"Well, you seem so determined now."

"Playing football for a living will be a lot more fun than being a garage mechanic," Mark said. "That's what I want."

"I suppose so," Anna said slowly, studying him. "What position do you play now?"

"I'm a lineman," Mark said. It was late fall now, and his breath made little puffs of smoke in the chilled air. "But I'm going to learn to throw passes pretty soon." He scraped his cleats against the walkway to underline what he said.

"That will be nice," Anna said. "I'll take some pictures of you. I've already got some from today's practice." She showed him her camera.

"I thought you were going to start making your own movies by now," Mark said.

"I *will*," Anna said, "as soon as I can save up the money for a motion picture camera."

"Well, it looks as though we're both sure of what we're going to be when we grow up," Mark said, smiling.

He waved good-bye to Anna and started toward the showers. He felt good. A few months ago he had been confused when Anna and the rest of the gang asked him about his future. Now he knew.

* * *

But was he *sure*?

One night, just as he was putting away a book about football, a thought struck him.

Mark knew he was good at playing football. After all, the coach had just put him on the second team. The second team members got to play if someone on the school's first team got tired or hurt. Getting on the second team already meant Mark was doing very well for his age, since this was just his first year.

But . . . did that mean he would ever get to be a quarterback?

Mark frowned. He didn't know. The future was hard to figure out.

"Mark! Come to supper," his mother called.

"Hurry up, superstar!" Claire shouted, laughing.

Mark walked in to supper, thinking.

"Dad?" he said after the meal had begun. "Can I go see your laboratory again tomorrow?"

His father looked up, surprised. "Well, I don't know. I'll be kind of busy tomorrow."

"Let him come," Mom said, serving some vegetables. "Not every boy's father has a time machine to look at."

Dad beamed. "You're right about that. Okay, Mark. Be at the laboratory tomorrow afternoon."

* * *

Mark didn't like the idea of sneaking another trip on his father's time machine. But his curiosity got the better of him. He wanted to *know* about the future, not just guess about it.

The laboratory was the same as before—gray cabinets and a bustle of activity. His father showed him some new equipment. The scientists were going to send several people into the future—*their* futures. That way they could piece together a picture of what the future would be like.

Of course, people who traveled forward in time might

not like what they saw. They might decide to change their futures by doing things differently. But even so, the basic things about the future should remain the same. That would be useful for the scientists to know.

Dad was showing Mark a new piece of equipment when someone called him away. Mark was interested in the instrument. It ticked and buzzed so hard he thought it might fall apart. But when his father started to leave, Mark saw his chance.

"I'll look around while you're gone, Dad," Mark called. His father nodded absentmindedly as he left.

Mark quickly made his way to the small booth. No one was working in the room. The lights on the control panel glowed.

He set the dials exactly the way he had before. He got in the booth and sat down. In the silence of the booth Mark could hear his pulse thumping in his ears. His hands felt cold and wet.

What would his future be like this time? It *had* to be different. He had stopped tinkering with engines, after all. That should change the future. He was sure now he wouldn't become a garage mechanic.

Now he was playing football. What would that lead to?

The booth hummed. Mark checked the laboratory clock.

2:26 P.M.

A buzz. Something clicked.

A sharp screech—

Pop.

* * *

Pop.

The booth was gone.

A distant buzz . . . cold air . . .

Clunk!

Something big hit him. Hard.

He tumbled over. His face slammed into the earth. He tasted mud.

Someone was lying on top of him. A shrill whistle blew in the chilly air.

"Hey!" Mark cried out.

"Okay, okay," came a gruff voice. "I hit you a little hard that time."

The weight lifted. Mark stared up into the face of a huge man in the pads and helmet of a football uniform.

I made it! Mark thought. *I'm a football player!*

A light rain drifted in the air. Mark could hear the distant *smack* and *thud* of bodies running into each other. He recognized them as the sounds of a football scrimmage. This was a practice session.

"C'mon, c'mon, on your feet." A big man in a coaching uniform moved into view. He stood over Mark, his hands on his hips.

Mark rolled over and stood up. He felt bulky in the uniform. He looked down. He wore an orange uniform. It was smeared with brown mud.

"Get in the line!" the coach yelled. "Move it!"

Mark glanced around. He was in a big stadium. The stands were empty. Men in football uniforms were practicing passing and kicking beneath a sky of smoky gray. A strange, blue, banana-shaped helicopter clattered by overhead.

"Hey! Mark!" the coach shouted. "You're not getting paid to daydream."

Mark shook his head to clear it and trotted over to the scrimmage line. His side had the ball. There was an empty space in the line between two bulky players.

Mark guessed that was his position. But the men were so big!

He dropped down into his playing crouch between the two men. Facing him was the defense. A huge man opposite Mark scowled at him and then hunched down, settling into the earth. On his helmet was his name—Owens.

Mark got into position too. When he glanced down, his own hands looked enormous. His legs were thick and they bulged with muscles. Mark felt a surge of pride. He was a big, powerful man, just like the others on the team.

The quarterback called out, "Thirty-seven, forty-two, six—hike!"

The center snapped the ball back to the quarterback.

Mark charged forward. Owens smacked into him.

Whoosh—the air rushed out of his lungs. Mark toppled backward.

Owens rolled over him and was through the tumbling pile of men before Mark could do anything. Owens dove forward and tackled the quarterback. They crashed to the ground. The ball popped out. It rolled away.

"Ball! Fumble!" somebody shouted.

One of Mark's teammates fell on it. Mark sucked in air. He was relieved that his side had kept the ball. He got to his feet, panting.

"What *happened* in there?" came the rough voice of the coach. Some of the team turned and looked at Mark.

"I missed him," Mark said simply. He was embarrassed. He noticed that his voice was deep. It seemed to come from farther down inside his chest.

"Okay," the coach said. "Let's try that play again. Quarterback, check your signals first."

Mark hunched down in the line again. He breathed deeply. He was determined to do better.

And he did. On the next play he stopped Owens with a solid block. The collision knocked the wind out of Mark again, but otherwise he was all right.

The afternoon went on. Mark hit the scrimmage line time and time again. He protected the quarterback while the quarterback threw pass after pass.

Mark's shoulders and knees and hips began to ache where he had been hit. He got used to tasting the muddy field. His orange uniform got so spattered with mud that he had to remember it had been orange before.

Mark grew tired. His eyes began to sting from sweat dripping down into them. He watched the quarterback make beautiful passes to other players down the field. But Mark was a replacement lineman, not a pass receiver. He was there to block, and that was all.

The rain fell harder. Mark slipped in the mud. Getting up from a scrimmage, he said to the coach, "Do we have to practice in a downpour?"

"What'll you do if it rains in a game," the coach said sarcastically. "Carry an umbrella to stay dry?"

Mark gritted his teeth and stood, hands on hips, waiting for the next play. Somehow this wasn't going the way he had thought it would. The sports stories he had read were different. They described how the hero made the crucial pass at the very end of the game and won the championship for his team. There wasn't anything at all in those stories about the guys who played in the line.

Mark wasn't sure he liked this part of football. Playing in the line was hard, and he never got to carry the ball. He was a replacement lineman, too, so he wasn't on the starting team. He would play in the game next Saturday only if somebody got injured.

Puffing, he gazed up at the buildings near the stadium. They didn't have very many windows. Mark wondered if that was to save energy. Probably people would have to save more energy in the future. Fewer windows meant less heat was lost in winter.

This was a strange world. Little things were different, like the tiny radio sets in the football helmets. Using the radios, a coach could talk to a player all the way across the field. It seemed like a good idea to Mark.

He peered up into the gray sky. The rain clouds

were blowing away. The sky slowly cleared. Mark thought about Anna. He wondered if she was making movies somewhere in this future.

A glimmer caught his eye. Far up in the sky he could see something twinkling. It was too big to be a star. A plane? No, it wasn't moving.

Mark suddenly realized he was seeing a space station. The silvery dot must be in orbit around the Earth!

Mark squinted to see. It was a tiny circle. *A spinning wheel in the sky,* Mark thought. *It must be huge! Wait until I tell Dad about this!*

But then Mark remembered that he couldn't tell Dad anything. He was sneaking this time-travel trip behind Dad's back.

"Get back in that line, you guys!" the coach called.

Mark nodded. His body felt heavy as he walked through the mud. *Squish squish,* his steps sounded. His left side was sore where he had fallen on it.

He saw Owens squatting down in the line. Mark made a sour grin at him and bent over. He wasn't looking forward to smashing into Owens again.

He crouched down in the mud and listened to the count. The pads on his shoulders rubbed against his wet skin.

"Six, seventeen . . ." the quarterback called out.

Mark squeezed his eyes tight.

"Hike!"

Pop.

* * *

Pop.

Nothing happened.

Owens didn't come crashing into him.

Mark opened his eyes.

The stadium was gone.

The lights of the laboratory beamed down. Mark felt warmer. He reached down and rubbed his legs. They seemed thin and small. But they weren't sore. And his shoulders didn't ache either.

A wave of relief washed over Mark. It felt wonderful to be back in a place he knew, and in a body that wasn't tired and hurt. He sat in the chair for a moment and enjoyed the feeling.

The clock on the wall said 2:27 P.M.

The laboratory door opened.

Mark's father walked in.

Mark jumped up. He stepped out of the time-travel booth.

"Trying it on for size?" Dad said.

"Well . . ." Mark didn't know what to say next.

"Wait a minute." His father frowned. Dad studied the dials on the front of the booth. Mark had not reset them.

"You've been on a time trip," his father said, surprised.

"Well, yes. . . I have."

His father scowled. "That was a very bad thing to do, Mark. It could be dangerous," he said in a serious tone.

"How?"

"Suppose the machine failed? Suppose it broke? Suppose you got stuck up there in the future and couldn't get back?"

"Well . . . it didn't break," Mark said.

His father's mouth pressed into a thin line. "If the time machine didn't bring you back, we would have no way to get you," he said.

Mark had never seen his father so angry. He looked down at his feet and tried to think of something to say.

"We are very careful here in the lab," his father said. "When we use this time machine we have many people standing by in case something goes wrong."

"Uh-huh," Mark muttered.

"You're a very lucky boy to be back here at all."

"I'm sorry, Dad. It seemed like a good idea."

"Well, it wasn't." His father's face relaxed a little. "Mark, I'll talk to you about this tonight, at home. Right now I want to check out the machine. Your trip may have damaged it."

"Okay, Dad."

"I'm disappointed in you, Mark."

Mark's face felt hot. "G'bye, Dad," he mumbled.

He left the laboratory, walking slowly. His eyes stung, but he blinked back the tears.

* * *

On the bus Mark watched the houses go by outside. Everything felt comfortable and familiar. The two different futures he had visited weren't like this. They felt strange, in a way he couldn't quite describe.

Inside himself Mark felt confused and sad. He didn't want to go home right away. The bus rumbled by his school. Classes were just ending. He saw some of his friends—Ron, Vanessa and Anna.

Mark suddenly got up and pulled the signal cord to stop the bus. At the next corner the bus wheezed to a stop. Mark got off. He walked back to the school and went inside.

Photography Club was beginning. It was the only place Mark felt like going. He made his way to the darkroom and rapped on the door. A voice called from inside, "Hold on a minute."

Mark paced back and forth outside. When Anna opened the door he asked, "Need any help?"

"Sure," Anna said. She looked glad to see him. "My pictures aren't coming out right. I don't understand what I'm doing wrong."

"Let me see."

Mark worked for a while with the film Anna was trying to develop.

"You have some interesting pictures here," Mark said. "But they're not clear."

He showed Anna how to put the sheets of developing paper in the trays. After waiting a few minutes he fished them out. The pictures were sharp and clear.

"That's great," Anna said happily.

It lifted Mark's spirits to be doing something he enjoyed. In the back of his mind was the memory of that football practice in the future. Before his time-travel trips Mark had been sure he would like to be a garage mechanic or a football player. But they hadn't turned out the way he expected. . . .

Mark pushed these thoughts aside. "Let's try this one," he said. He rolled more of Anna's film on a projector. He clicked a switch. "That's an important step," he said. "The projector puts the picture onto this developing paper."

"That's easy," Anna said. "I can do that. But getting them developed . . . "

Mark swirled the developing fluid around in the tray. Anna's photograph showed a tree with lacy clouds above it. The picture slowly cleared. Mark studied it in the dim, red light of the darkroom. Something about the shadows among the tree limbs caught his eye. He took the photo out of the tray.

"Hey!" Anna cried out. "My picture isn't sharp yet!"

Mark hung it up to dry. "I know. It looks better this way."

"I thought we were always supposed to get our pictures as clear as possible," Anna said.

"I don't think so," Mark said. He pointed at the dripping sheet. "See these fuzzy branches. They're more interesting to look at than ordinary tree branches. And see those clouds? They look like cotton."

"Ummmmmm," Anna said, squinting at the photograph. "I . . . I think I see what you mean. It's *prettier* this way."

She turned to Mark. "You should do this when you grow up, Mark. You're really *good* at seeing interesting things in pictures."

"But my sister said machines develop all the pictures," Mark said.

"Did she?" Anna tossed her head to dismiss the idea. Her pigtails bounced. "Well, she doesn't know about *artistic* pictures, dummy. You could develop the artistic movies I'm going to make."

Mark smiled. One of the things he liked about Anna was how she was so sure of everything she said. It made her funny sometimes, too.

* * *

That evening his father asked Mark to go for a walk before supper. They puffed as they climbed to the top of a hill near their house. Then they stood looking out over their town. The sun was a dim, orange glow in the west.

"I talked to your mother," Dad said. "We think we know why you used the time machine."

"I wanted to find out what I'd be when I grew up," Mark said quietly.

"Right." Dad nodded.

"I certainly did find out," Mark said, and sighed. He felt tired. A lot had happened that day.

"You found out what you *could* become, Mark. Not what you *must* become."

"But Dad—" Then Mark told his father about the garage and why he didn't like working there. Dad just nodded. He was interested when Mark described the chimpanzees and how they worked.

When his father asked about the second time trip, Mark described the stadium and what it felt like to work as a football player. Mark mentioned the space station and how it looked like a giant wheel in the sky.

"How big did it seem?" his father asked.

"Oh . . . about as big as a dime held at arm's length," Mark said.

"Good grief. That's *enormous*."

"Maybe I should be a scientist like you, Dad. That way I could get to work on that space station when I grow up. Then I could—"

He stopped, because Dad was chuckling. "You made those kind of plans about playing football when you grew up, too," Dad said.

"Well, gee, I was wrong about football, Dad. That doesn't mean I'm wrong about being a scientist."

"Son, there are good things and bad things about every job. Being a garage mechanic isn't always fun. Neither is being a football player. Or a scientist."

"Well . . . yes . . . I guess."

"You can't just take the good parts and leave the bad ones."

Mark frowned. "Dad? You *invented* the time machine. Have you gone on a time trip yourself?"

"No."

"Why not?"

His father put his hands in his pockets and kicked a rock down the hillside. It thumped and bounced from view. "I'm interested in the future, sure," Mark's father said. "Everybody is. But it isn't so important to me what I'll be doing in fifteen years. What's important is what my life is like *now*. The present is interesting enough."

Mark remembered Anna's photograph. Sometimes things were better if they weren't sharp and clear.

"Dad, I'm sorry about sneaking trips in your time machine. It's . . . it's just that everybody was asking me what I wanted to be, and . . . " Mark stopped, blinking. Below, the yellow lights of the town were winking on.

"Son, never mind how things will turn out. The question to ask yourself is What do you like doing right now?"

Mark smiled, thinking about all that had happened since that day in the schoolyard, with Anna and her movies and all the rest of the gang. Mark realized that he had never really asked himself Dad's question. Instead, he had tried to guarantee his future. He wanted to "program" his future like a computer.

"I think you'll find one step at a time is quite enough," Dad said quietly.

"One step in *this* time," Mark said, smiling. "And let the future take care of itself."

About the Authors

CHARLES DE LINT is a Canadian novelist, poet, short story writer, and folk musician whose work in the fantasy field has won him awards and prizes. Among his novels for adults are MOONHEART, RIDDLE OF THE WREN, and YARROW.

PATRICIA C. WREDE, who lives in Minnesota, has written several fantasy novels. One, for young adults, is TALKING TO DRAGONS, for which her story in this volume is a kind of prequel, which means it happened *before* the events of the novel take place.

BRUCE COVILLE is so energetic, he once sold six novels in a single day. He is the author of the fast-paced sf mystery series about the A1 Gang, and his book for young readers, THE MONSTER'S RING, will be shown on *CBS Storybreak*. He also writes musical plays and sings and acts, mostly around Syracuse, New York, where he lives.

ROBERT LAWSON, who died in 1957, left several unpublished short stories, of which "The Silver Leopard" is one.

Best known for his children's books BEN & ME and RABBIT
HILL, and his drawings for Munro Leaf's THE STORY OF
FERDINAND, Lawson is the only individual to win both the
Newbery Medal (for RABBIT HILL) and the Caldecott Medal
(for THEY WERE STRONG AND GOOD).

ANNE ELIOT CROMPTON, who lives in western Massachusetts, has a broad writing ability. She has written
picture books (THE WINTER WIFE), historical novels (THE
SORCERER), puppet plays, and adult books as well.

ISAAC ASIMOV is one of the most prolific writers in the
world, having written well over 200 books. His stories have
been translated into many different languages, and he writes
monthly columns for two of America's best-known science
fiction/fantasy magazines. Dr. Asimov lives in New York
City. His books in the FOUNDATION series have been on the
best-seller lists for months at a time.

BARRY B. LONGYEAR has many award-winning stories
and novels in print, but perhaps his most famous is an award-
winning short story called "Enemy Mine," which was made
into a feature movie. He lives in Maine and is in great
demand as a teacher of writing.

ELYSE GUTTENBERG, who lives in Alaska, is a poet
who has been widely published in magazines and who serves
on the Alaska State Arts Council. "Selena's Song" is her
first published short story.

JANE YOLEN, president of the Science Fiction Writers
of America, has written over ninety books, many of them
award-winning fantasy novels and fairy tale collections, such
as THE GIRL WHO CRIED FLOWERS, the Pit Dragon Trilogy,
and the ever-popular Commander Toad books. She lives in
Hatfield, Massachusetts.

ELIZABETH S. HELFMAN is best known for her non-fiction books for young readers, which have garnered her many prizes, including the Golden Kite Award for BLIS-SYMBOLICS. She lives in Connecticut.

JOHN FORRESTER is the pseudonym for a young adult novelist and short story writer who lives in Massachusetts. As Forrester, he has written a science fiction trilogy that begins with BESTIARY MOUNTAIN.

JESSICA AMANDA SALMONSON, who lives in Seattle, is well known as a novelist for adults. She has published a series of books about a mythical Japan called Nippon where magic works. Like her heroine Tomoe Gozen, Ms. Salmonson is a martial arts expert. She also publishes books and magazines of horror tales and poems.

GREGORY BENFORD is a physicist at the University of California and a prize-winning novelist of such books as the Nebula Award-winning TIMESCAPE and ACROSS THE SEA OF SUNS. This is his first story for children.